Carol Bruggen

HALF
THE GLADNESS

ANDRE DEUTSCH

All the characters in this novel are fictitious
and any resemblance to actual persons, living or dead,
is therefore coincidental.

First published 1985 by
André Deutsch Limited
105 Great Russell Street London WC1

Bruggen, Carol
Half the gladness.
I. Title
823'.914[F]   PR6052.R7/

ISBN 0–233–97757–0

Phototypeset by Falcon Graphic Art Ltd,
Wallington, Surrey
Printed in Great Britain by
Ebenezer Baylis & Son Ltd, Worcester

For Gwendolyn Mary with love
and for Poppy, remembering.

We look before and after,
  And pine for what is not:
Our sincerest laughter
  With some pain is fraught;
Our sweetest songs are those that tell
  of saddest thought.

. . . .

Teach me half the gladness
  That thy brain must know,
Such harmonious madness
  From my lips would flow
The world should listen then – as I am
  listening now.

From 'To a Skylark'
by Percy Bysshe Shelley

1

'Good afternoon, your worship,' said Frances to the Mayor.

'I see you've had your ears lowered,' he replied. He pulled at his own just visible beneath a luxuriant growth of grey whiskers and smiled ruefully. 'Just washed mine. Can't do anything with them.'

'I like your hair cut short, too,' he added as an after-thought.

It's only a small matter. But they are all only small matters.

The sun was drawing heat as if out of the melted tarmac on the village street. The worn paving stones glowed. Outside the cottages geraniums and roses bloomed. A sky as blue and solid as the Mediterranean sat on the hills, sending shivers of haze horizontally among the trees.

Why can't it all be like this.

It is all like this.

The Mayor saluted her as she hurried past Hermione's gate and went into her own garden.

'Watch out for the trams,' he advised, 'they're sending out duplicates today.'

It was the Mayor's fond hope that one day a tram would appear in the village.

She couldn't remember the day she was born. But she could remember things that had happened not long after. She could remember, for instance, when her brother was born.

In those days, in that sphere of society, it was not acceptable to mention anything connected with babies. It was certainly not thought that previous children would need to know that a brother or sister was about to appear on the scene. Parents were not imbeciles. Even from less intelligent children one could expect to have questions asked which would lead to the connection between a baby and the bulge in the unmentionable abdomen. With more intelligent ones one might even anticipate the awful horror of the question,

'How did it get there?'

To avoid this the only course was to avoid the subject until after the event and then let Nanny have the problem. That was what she was paid for.

Frances was taken with Celia and Keith to the expensive nursing home where her mother was ill.

'How are you, my dear?' George beamed.

Radiant, clad in a pale blue negligee with feathers, Hermione surveyed her brood.

'Pull your knickers up, Frances,' she said.

'Under the bed, look under the bed,' suggested George hurriedly.

Under the bed they found a crate of peaches.

'One each,' Hermione commanded.

It was while they were eating their peaches that Frances noticed the blue wicker cradle at the foot of her mother's bed. Inside it a fat pink baby was lying with its fists curled up in front of its mouth, fast asleep.

'And how is the little fellow?' asked George.

'Oh, he's wonderful – a wonderful baby. No trouble to feed. Sleeps right through the night,' Hermione replied.

It occurred to Frances that her mother didn't look very ill.

The three children stood round the cradle and contemplated its occupant.

With the instinct of all normal three-year-olds Frances put her hand in the cot and felt the little cheek with her forefinger.

'Don't touch the baby,' said her mother sharply.

Celia gazed at the floor. Keith chuckled. Frances felt the taste of peach changing into the taste of hatred.

They are all only small matters.

It's just that a lifetime of them seems to take some of the sparkle out of summer.

The telephone was ringing.

As she hurried to answer it Frances thought it might be Albert.

'Hello Gorgeous,' said the voice at the other end of the telephone.

'Would you have said that if it had been the Queen Mother?'

'Most certainly,' replied Albert. 'Only the other day when I had dialled your number and she answered I greeted her like that. "Albert," she said, "please lower your voice. Nobody else knows I'm here. They think I'm at the Chelsea Flower Show." '

'I see. So you do knock about with other women when I'm not at home.'

'Yes. But I'm choosy. And it's a nice day so we'll go and paint those trees that we saw up by the reservoir when it was raining.'

Albert's paintings were realistic and imaginative at the same time. Of course, you had to interpret. But Albert had a way of interpreting that still left you with a vision of what was actually there. When Frances interpreted, things changed out of recognition.

Perhaps that is the answer, she thought. Perhaps it is a kind of mental astigmatism that makes what other people see seem different to me.

Under the trees there were thousands of mosquitoes. Midges, in England. Once you have met a mosquito you tend to think that everything pestilential is related to it directly.

In Canada they ate Aunt Clara as if there were no tomorrow.

Albert settled himself on the other side of the river and began to draw, a spare pencil tucked under the rim of his hat, a look of profound contentment on his wrinkled face.

Glancing at him over the top of her easel Frances realised that he had forgotten she was there. She lit a cigarette to discourage the midges, squeezed crimson, black, ochre, blue and yellow around one part of the old plate she used as a palette and put a large lump of flake white on the space that was left.

Aunt Clara had in fact been eaten by everything: by her sister Hermione, by the four-year-old Nigel which emerged in time from that blue wicker cradle, by Frances, by her love for humanity, and ultimately by her own liver in its protest against the quantities of whisky, or Scotch as they called it in Canada, that she had lavished upon it.

'Sam,' Aunt Clara would say to her beaky husband, 'Sam, I'm mad at you.' Bang. She would close the screen door which led on to the front porch so that the trailing blossoms leapt about in panic and she would go out into the evening air and commune with her flowers until she felt better.

If Aunt Clara had been my mother instead of Hermione things would have been different. Of course they would have been different. They would have been different. That was about as logical as saying that if things had been different they would have been different. And about as much use, Frances thought.

She began to block in the sky, using a large brush with a broken end which had been strapped up with a piece of sticking plaster. The midges stuck to the paint and were struggling everywhere, on her hardboard, on her palette, on the end of her brush. She sighed. Everything she did became a problem.

She glanced across at Albert. He was working steadily, measuring, screwing up his eyes against the sun, filling his page with pencil marks, swift and sure, before applying the watercolours.

Albert was an observer. He watched the colours of the hills. He noticed the changes in the sky, the way the landscape moved back from focal points and was submerged by light, the shifting signs of the seasons. All these things filled him with delight.

Once he had been describing emotions in terms of a river, talking about the way the water changes from shallow and shiny to deep, black and still, to waterfalls, to movement and laughter over rocks, through channels with steep sides where it becomes transparent and glowing until it reaches the sea.

'Albert, you are a poet,' Frances had exclaimed.

'No,' he had replied, 'I'm not a poet. I'm just someone who observes rivers.'

To be with Albert was to be whole. He noticed everything. He knew when she was agitated and needed to be calmed. He knew when she was subdued and needed a joke. He knew when she wanted to be reminded of her father, George. He knew when she wanted to be a woman. He knew when she wanted to be his mother. He knew when she wanted the family warmth that he generated so well and when she wanted the isolation and tranquillity of the moors. He knew everything about her. He knew everything about everything.

But according to the rules, according to Hermione's rules, Albert should have had no place in her life.

2

According to Hermione's rules the only people to have places in other people's lives were those who had a licence, and who had a licence was determined by rules. You had a licence if you were related by blood. You had a licence if you were related by marriage, proper marriage, that is, not any of your registry office or love marriages. You had a licence if you were being paid for.

So it was that all the people in Celia, Keith, Frances and Nigel's early childhood had a licence, most of them on the grounds that they were being paid for.

'Can I have another piece of bread and jam?' Frances had asked Nanny.

'Please may I . . .' Nanny corrected.

'Please may I have another piece of bread and jam?'

'No jam on the last piece,' Nanny reminded her.

'How do I know it is going to be my last piece?' she enquired.

That is how the British became British. That is how they became the most illogical and eccentric nation in the world. It was all brought about by generations of silver-haired ladies with a bellyful of axioms culled from the Bible, and generations of genuine mothers and grandmothers. It was no good questioning the wisdom of these axioms. They were the *status quo*; knowledge or ignorance of them made the difference between being middle class and the rest.

Hermione had a great distrust of the rest. She had only one strong motive which in its turn motivated all her other motives. This was that she should be recognised as the superior person that she felt herself to be.

Albert, brought up in a sprawling family, knew more of these axioms than Frances did.

'Get rid of that man who hangs about in your kitchen,' Hermione commanded one day.

Albert made love with astonishing ease. Perhaps it was because each of them had so many things to forget. Perhaps it was because if marriages aren't made in heaven, as Nanny and Albert's mother would have said, love affairs are. Perhaps it was simply because their chemistry was right. Whatever it was Frances felt that she was wasting her time when she and Albert weren't making love. He brought back the sparkle to the summer. He brought the smell of the bracken and the streams, the sounds of the skylarks, the heat of the sun. When he smiled at her and she smiled at him it was as if all the joyous things of the world which get forgotten in the shindy of living came out of their hiding places like small creatures, tentative at first and then bolder and sure of themselves in the forest. She held him in her arms and he growled softly and she growled back at him. It saved the trouble and misunderstanding of speech. The growls which spoke and answered each other amused them both and expressed emotions which neither would have tried to commit to mere words. They were silly. They were both silly, silly with love, silly with the happiness of drifting into each other as the rainbow colours over splashing water drift into each other.

But Albert didn't have a licence to drift into Frances, and she had no licence to drift into him.

When Hermione first discovered Albert sitting at the kitchen table in her daughter's house she saw at once that he was out of place. She recognised his tall, thin shape as that of an ordinary man, which under the circumstances was a remarkable feat. Albert, after all, did not look ordinary. He had a brown, weatherbeaten face and an overgrown silver moustache which curled round his mouth like a contented cat. Also, he always wore an ancient bush hat with a hole in its crown. If Hermione had been paying Albert to do something for her she would have found him valuable. Although before he retired he had been an inspector for the corporation bus service, Albert could turn his hand to anything. As somebody sitting in the kitchen drinking tea and being adored, however, she felt that he should be got rid of.

Frances, the younger daughter of Hermione, was married to somebody else. Frances was married to William, and goodness knows he put up with enough from her without having it be known in the village that his wife was having an unlicensed love affair.

Aunt Clara, if she had not been eaten by her liver and had not lived in Canada on the other side of the Atlantic Ocean, would have understood. Aunt Clara was different.

3

As the afternoon advanced the air became cooler and the midges ceased to dance under the trees where Frances was sitting and made their way down to the water. On her easel the picture was taking shape, or as much shape as paintings by Frances took. Albert was filling his water jar at the stream. He was leaning as far over as he could to reach a clear, deep patch without falling in. His hat was pushed back on his head. When his hat was on the back of his head he was Slam, ace reporter. Frances was Slim, his secretary. As Slim and Slam they had observed many interesting events from the front seat of Albert's car, or from the hillsides when they were walking. Once they had noticed two runners preparing themselves, putting on their training shoes, their tracksuits and bands around their foreheads and setting off together at a comfortable jog. Half an hour later the woman had returned without the man, very red in the face and out of breath. She had climbed into the car out of which they had emerged when they arrived and changed her clothes. Slam rose to the bait.

'Looks like a bad case to me. Did you notice blood on the left training shoe? Behind those trees over there to the right. She waited until he reached the lower path along the bank of the river. Then she took a rock to him. Threw the body in the river. It should be coming downstream any time now.'

In the interests of public order and justice they had waited for an hour until the missing person returned, also very red in the face, having taken a longer route than his companion.

It is surprising how many crimes never take place.

'Pity about that,' Slam mumbled gloomily as the second

runner climbed into the car and rejoined his friend. 'It was developing well. Another scoop down the drain.'

He filled his water jar and Frances noticed that he was wearing brown socks with green diamonds on the ankles. They were the ones she had mended for him last winter.

He wandered back to his drawing board and glanced up across the stream at Frances. They had not spoken for an hour and a half.

The air seemed to be as green as the summer leaves under her trees. The hillside was dry and brown with the crumbly, warm soil smelling like Stockwell's greenhouse. Stockwell had been one of Hermione and George's paid licensees. He was, in fact, the gardener at the big house to which the blue wicker cradle containing Nigel had been taken when Hermione had recovered from her 'illness' and the others had begun to realise that they had a new brother.

'Would you like some coffee?' Albert called and his voice was muffled by the heat and the midges and the murmuring stream and the long grass and the ferns and the thick piles of fallen branches and summer in general.

It was all so lovely.

The Mayor would be surprised if he could see Frances now. He probably thought when he met her coming back from the shop that she would be starting to make the tea for William.

In any case, if he had known that she was going to the moors with Albert he would have conjectured otherwise than that they were going out to paint.

'Aye-aye,' he would have said, 'another rambling rose rambling.' Just as he always referred to the dead whose names appeared in the obituary column of the local paper as 'another that has given up smoking'.

They sat under the tree and drank Albert's coffee. He had a huge flask which could keep them going all day.

Frances thought about life.

If Albert and I were married we could fill the flask in the morning and spend every day like this. In the winter we would find places with heating to look at, the old churches and cathedrals, the museums and antique shops which abound in this area. In the summer it would always be like this.

There would be no news bulletins, no newspapers, no international crises, no threat of ultimate destruction.

It is all here. We have all the ingredients for a very nice world.

The world is a village. We had a very nice village, too.

Albert put his arms around her. Some schoolboys passing along the moorland road in a minibus leant out of its windows and shouted cheerfully,

'Leave 'er alone, mister.'

4

While Albert and Frances were enjoying the summer under the trees by the brook and the Mayor was haymaking in his underpants, having gone back to his farm after seeing Frances in the village street on his way to procure the day's allotment of rum – rum being his little failing – further up the hill Joan was having a quarter of an hour with her neighbour Alice.

They were sitting in Alice's kitchen drinking mugs of coffee while their various children disported themselves unsupervised, Joan having taken a few minutes off, Alice having, as usual, no very clear idea as to the whereabouts or activities of her three.

'There's water coming through the ceiling, Alice, dear,' said Joan, looking up. Her short, straight hair shone, neat and ordered like her tidy mind. It contrasted sharply with Alice's long brown pigtail which always appeared to be trying to escape from its fastening, as her thoughts were always trying to escape from whatever bounds she put on them.

'Water?' Alice's mental sorting paraphernalia began to grind. Her store of ideas, huge as a hot air balloon, tight with the resources of thousands of books and utterly bereft of ropes to hold it down, began to strain in the atmosphere.

'Yes, dear. See, it's dripping on to the floor.'

Alice's kitchen was below the level of the road. Above it, where the front door had been in centuries gone by, was the sitting room. Above the sitting room, on the third floor, were the children's bedroom and the bathroom.

'Water,' mused Alice, peering into her coffee. 'I expect it's just water.'

'Yes, dear, it's water.' Joan, like everyone else in the village, was used to explaining practical matters to Alice. 'But it shouldn't be coming through the ceiling.'

Hadrian, Alice's eldest son, appeared in the kitchen doorway.

'Hello, Hadrian, my love.' Alice held out her arms to him.

Hadrian avoided her embrace and sat down on the floor.

'Hadrian,' Joan ventured, 'have you been playing in the bathroom?'

Hadrian nodded, a pleased expression on his face.

'They are much nearer to water at their age than we are,' explained Alice defensively. Then she brightened up. 'Have you made a lovely river in the washbasin, petal?'

Hadrian nodded again and removed his shoes.

In the middle of the kitchen floor a pool was forming.

Alice pushed her chair back a foot to avoid it.

Joan stood up.

'Hadrian,' she said, 'do you remember taking the plug out of the basin before you made your river?'

Hadrian gave her a bountiful smile and tried to float his right shoe across the lake on the pine boards.

'Alice, I think perhaps we should investigate. I mean, it's coming down two floors.'

'Hadrian, petal, just run up and stop the river, there's a good chap,' murmured Alice, sipping her coffee and curling her feet up on to the bar of the chair above the Ganges.

Hadrian had found that as his shoe was wet and heavy it would not float. He disappeared into the next room and came back with a plastic battleship which he steered backwards and forwards across the widening seascape.

'Perhaps I'd better go, Alice dear,' said Joan, heading for the first narrow flight of stairs. On the second floor the water was coming through the ceiling in a steady flow. The sitting-room carpet had a dark patch in its centre, the coloured wool flattened in little whirlpools where streams of water hit it.

Joan raised the edge of the carpet and worked a stool under its damp weight until it stood beneath the Niagara, raising the carpet from the floor so that the downpour was deflected in a kind of fountain.

Then she flew up the second flight of stairs and gazed into the bathroom.

The linoleum was holding its own. Water poured over the sides of the washbasin and rested, quietly searching for a way back to ground level, an inch and a half deep from wall to wall. Both taps were on full.

Alice appeared behind her.

'Oh, hasn't he had a lovely time. Look at all his little ships. The Trojan fleet. *And* it is warm. You see, the water he was playing in is warm. So significant.' She trailed her hands in the embryonic ocean.

'It'll be significant if the ceiling collapses.' Joan waded through the Trojan fleet towards the washbasin. She turned off the taps and pulled out the plug. With a great gurgle the water sped down the hole, and Joan began to soak up the flood with a towel which she wrung out repeatedly over the bath.

Alice stood in the receding tide with watermarks over the ankles of her jeans.

Hadrian was a quiet child. Endymion, Alice's next, who was a year younger, tended to get into mischief.

'I wonder what Endymion is doing,' said Joan.

They climbed back down the narrow staircases hearing the rallentando of the waters as they went.

5

'Have you smelt the drains?' Hermione demanded from her front gate as Frances and Albert drew up in Albert's car.

'It's the hot weather, Mrs Tattersall,' said Albert. 'Can't expect anything else in this heat.'

'Hot weather, rubbish. In Canada the summers are scorching and the drains don't smell. It's your sink, Frances. I keep telling you not to put things down it. Tea leaves. Rice. Disgusting. You are poisoning the drains. Think of the rats.'

'I'd rather not think of the rats,' said Frances, removing her wet painting from the boot of Albert's car and standing it against the wall.

'I've been right up the hill and they are all the same. Every one of them. As soon as you bend down you can smell them.'

'Most of us don't bend down to smell the drains,' Frances objected mildly.

She had thought and felt, at times, that the bad state of the whole world was due to her. So good a job had Hermione made of bringing up her younger daughter that Frances felt responsible for everything that went wrong with everyone. But it never occurred to her before that she was encouraging the rats in the sewers. Here was something else to think about during the long nights when William was away at those conferences.

'They breed, you know,' Hermione continued.

'What breeds, Mother?' Frances was extricating her paint-brushes from some branches she had collected to decorate the kitchen.

'Everything breeds.' Hermione was indignant. 'The rats breed. The germs breed.'

'I thought you meant the rice and the tea leaves bred.'

'Well, they cause it all, don't they? I mean, if you didn't put rice and tea leaves down your sink the rats wouldn't have anything to eat. Then they wouldn't breed.'

'Do they only eat rice and tea leaves?' Frances gathered up her painting plate and her oil and turpentine and went into her house.

Albert closed the boot of his car and looked thoughtful.

'Very hard to stop, Mrs Tattersall,' he announced at length.

'What is hard to stop?' Hermione looked at him accusingly.

'Breeding's hard to stop, Mrs Tattersall,' he concluded. 'It's very hard to stop things breeding.'

'Rubbish. Of course it isn't. Hygiene is the answer. Rice and tea leaves should go in a polythene bag in the dustbin.'

'Make the dustbin smell, in this heat,' Albert pointed out.

'Don't mumble Mr . . . er . . .' Hermione had been told Albert's name many times but she chose to be unable to remember it.

'Halstead, Mrs Tattersall. I said, it would make the dustbin smell, putting rice and tea leaves into it in this hot weather. Better off down the drain.'

'The dustbin gets emptied.' Hermione spoke as if she were addressing Endymion, to whom she had always spoken in a disapproving voice since the day she discovered him peeing against the hydrangea shrub in the tub in her front yard.

'Aye. But the drain gets washed.' Albert's voice was quiet and thoughtful.

'I know that you and Frances are friends but there is no need to defend her unreasonably. The fact is, the state of these drains is deplorable. I shall write to the council.'

'Been like it a long time, I shouldn't wonder,' mused Albert. 'Never heard of a plague in these parts.' He carried the wet painting into the house, holding it carefully with his palms pressed against its edges.

Hermione followed him.

'And there's another thing,' she announced.

It was dark in the kitchen after the bright sunlight outside.

Albert filled the kettle and plugged it in. He emptied the tea leaves out of the teapot into the sink and rinsed it under the tap.

'Don't you think it's been a beautiful afternoon?' Frances said to nobody in particular.

'That wood outside your back door,' Hermione continued.

'It's attracting the rabbits,' Frances suggested.

'Don't be silly, dear. That wood has been piled up there ever since I came to live next door to you. Isn't it about time somebody moved it? It could fall on someone.'

'That wood has been there for twenty years,' said Frances.

'Then it is time it went. Ask William to move it.'

'You ask William to move it. I stopped asking William to move it fifteen years ago. I'm getting rather fond of it.'

'Would you like a cup of tea, Mrs Tattersall?' asked Albert.

'No thank you, Mr . . . er . . .' Hermione replied. I never have tea after four o'clock. Well, I'll mention it to him then. He might move it for me.'

The implication that William would find Hermione's request reasonable when the same request from his wife was not didn't escape Frances.

Albert took two mugs out of the cupboard and filled them with tea. He added milk from the bottle, stirred four spoonfuls of sugar into each and offered Frances a cigarette.

The implication in Albert's studied tea preparations that she was not wanted did not escape Hermione.

She went back to her own cottage, whamming her daughter's front door closed like a clap of thunder.

6

After Albert had gone home Frances picked up a potato and began to peel it.

If it had just been the baby there would have been no problem.

But the command negated so much that the baby epitomised.

The fact that she and William were childless had nothing to do with Hermione. She was sure of that. William would have hated being a father. And she, absent-minded as she was, would certainly have left babies lying around at railway stations and in shops. She would never have known where they were. She would probably not even have recognised them when they were restored to her.

The doorbell rang.

With the potato in one hand and a tea towel in the other Frances went to answer it.

'I must talk to you. I have to talk to someone and I thought to myself, "Frances will be in. Frances will listen to me."'

It was the Mayor's sister, Thelma.

'Oh, come in and have a cup of tea, Thelma,' said Frances happily, putting the half-peeled potato back into the vegetable rack, filling the kettle and emptying the teapot which still contained the remains of Albert's tea ceremony.

Thelma's face was swollen and her eyes had shrunken into their sockets as if she had been made of some plastic material which somebody had squeezed before it had set.

'It's my Howard. He's gone for good this time. He's left me and I don't know whether to be glad or sorry.' Thelma sat down beside the kitchen table and took a wad of wet tissues from the pocket of her cotton dress.

Frances handed her a few sheets of paper towel and she dabbed them distractedly against her receding eyes.

A faint anxiety that these would be totally absorbed by the paper towel and that she would be left with Thelma's puffy, eyeless face struck Frances.

'Oh dear,' she observed, upset by this thought and by Thelma's distress.

'Yes. I knew it would happen one day. I knew it was only a matter of time. He's always been a sucker for women. Small men are, you know. It makes them feel bigger. I liked him small but I suppose they do too. This one had him lined up from the moment she saw him pushing the trolley in Leo's Superstore. Some of them do that, you know,' she explained.

'He was doing the Saturday shopping.' Frances fell in with the picture, seeing Howard cheerfully filling his trolley with cornflakes and margarine being swooped down upon by a Valkyrie.

'Yes,' Thelma assented, 'they get themselves all organised with a good job and a house and no money worries and then they find that there is something missing. So they hang about looking for a mature man with a few children and a wife who thinks he'd like a bit on the side. It seems to give them a little kick, destroying somebody's hard-earned security.' She looked at Frances who handed her a cup of tea and sat down by the table taking one of her friend's trembling hands.

'Now let's forget about the feelings for the moment and look at the practical aspects,' she suggested, gazing into the small remains of Thelma's eyes as if by the power of her own gaze she could draw them back to the surface. 'Has he left you any money?'

'None at all. I have a few pounds of the housekeeping. There's nothing in the bank and we have the gas bill to pay. Fortunately it's not very big because it's been so hot. But what do I do next? How am I going to look after two children with no money and no job?'

With a desperate thrashing of the imagination Frances

tried to put herself in Thelma's position, to understand her sense of rejection, her fury, her feeling of injustice and her hopelessness.

She failed.

'Well,' she said comfortably, 'I'll give you some money to tide you over, and you must find a lawyer. He can't just leave you like that without anything. He has to look after you. You are his wife.'

Thelma stopped sobbing and wiped her nose which, unlike her eyes, seemed to be growing bigger as a result of the conflict within.

'I knew you'd help,' she said, 'but I can't afford a lawyer. And I can't live on charity.' She drank her tea. Her mouth, Frances noted with relief, looked about its usual size.

'What about your brother? He must have a lawyer.' The Mayor, a bachelor farmer, would surely know what to do to assist.

'Oh, I daren't tell him. He never liked my Howard. Said he was a prat. I suppose I'll have to stop calling him "my Howard". He's her Howard now. He'd go and find out where they are living. He's got a shotgun, you know. For the rats. He'd stop at nothing.'

A confused vision of the Mayor, with his beard flowing and his shotgun at the ready, leaving his hayfield, furious in his underpants, surrounded by the thousands of rats which had waxed fat on the rice and tea leaves that she had allowed into the sewers, in pursuit of Thelma's Howard paralysed her mind and Frances sat in silence for a moment waiting for it to stir again before she replied,

'Well, I'll ask William when he comes home. I think you can get legal help free if you can't afford to pay for it. He knows about things like that. Meanwhile, if I give you ten pounds that will help for a day or two.'

'Oh, you mustn't,' said Thelma, gratefully stuffing the two five-pound notes Frances withdrew from her purse down the front of her dress into one side of her bra. 'I'll pay you back as soon as it gets settled. It's just that I don't know where to turn.'

'No, that's a present. We've been friends for a long time,

Thelma, and I know you'd do the same for me,' Frances replied, thinking that William having a good job, the house being paid for and there being no children, she came in the same category as the lady who had stolen Howard. Though she, Frances, would never destroy a family. Albert was a widower. 'You never know, he might be back in a week. He might not be able to stand the pace.'

They smiled at each other.

Thelma's eyes were a bit nearer the front now, and her nose had subsided.

When she had gone Frances took the half-peeled potato out of the vegetable rack and wondered why it was that some people had such excruciatingly difficult lives, while others, like herself, had no problems at all.

Except for Hermione.

But Hermione had not left her with children and bills and no money.

As she picked up the potato peelings which had fallen off the draining board Frances wondered vaguely what sort of a mother had produced the Mayor and Thelma.

'Lots of axioms, lots and lots of axioms,' she murmured to herself, putting the potatoes she had peeled into the refrigerator and then remembering that she had intended to put them on the stove.

7

'Whaddaya want, Nigel? Whaddaya want, honey?' Aunt Clara had said to her distressed nephew.

He was sitting on the windowsill looking out at the bright

army of hollyhocks which marched along the fence under the stern eye of the commanding poplar trees.

It was August 1940. They had arrived in Canada suffering from the measles. Now the measles had subsided and the curtains had been drawn back in the darkened bedroom. They were about to embark on an adventure, an adventure which made travelling across the Atlantic on a ship filled with evacuees and surrounded by corvettes on the lookout for enemy U-boats pale as the white peonies were pale beside the crimson tunics of the hollyhocks.

'I want the potty,' Nigel replied tearfully.

Aunt Clara had no cook, no nanny, no housekeeper, no gardener, just a little French daily who spoke no English and had crossed eyes.

'Wal, now.' Aunt Clara pondered.

George had remembered the 1914–18 war. He had armed himself with a knobkerrie taken from the wall of the big panelled entrance hall and prepared to repel the Bosche as they descended by parachute on and around Pendle Hill.

He did not want to be encumbered with children, following and getting underfoot while he was about it. So, in response to the request of Hermione's sisters who had been demanding that they should be sent for some months, the children had gone.

Frances had thought that it would not be for long. When the Germans saw George's knobkerrie appearing over the crest of Pendle they would certainly surrender. He would swing it round his head. It was a fearsome weapon, made of very heavy, black, polished wood and elaborately carved.

'Badly,' Nigel persisted.

Aunt Clara looked at her sister's baby. She said casually,

'How about it? How about trying the toilet now that you are a big strong fella again?'

Nigel who was not quite five was missing his nanny. While he had been sick and lost with the measles he had not noticed that it was Aunt Clara who was attending to these delicate matters. Now, in the sunshine of the bedroom, his sensitivities were once more sharp and edgy.

'I want the potty.' His face was fixed in an expression of agonised obduracy.

Aunt Clara was in a dilemma. She had been becoming concerned about the absence of bowel activity in Nigel's potty productions. Yet she felt that a child of his age should be able to use the lavatory.

'It's coming,' said Nigel ominously.

Aunt Clara lifted him hurriedly and carried him to the bathroom. She began to undo his buttons.

'I'll do it myself,' Nigel declared, 'but I want the potty.'

At the end of Aunt Clara's bathroom there was an airing cupboard without a door. At one side of it stood the hot-water cylinder. At the other, wooden racks for drying rose to the ceiling. Under these there was a small dark space.

Nigel pointed to the space.

'And I want it in there.' He was beginning to get very red in the face.

Aunt Clara ran and fetched the chamber pot from the bedroom and installed it in the darkened recess of the airing cupboard.

There, in solitary splendour, Nigel for the first time in his life removed his own trousers and sat meditating as he responded to the satisfying movement of his bowels.

'Well, did you ever,' Aunt Clara exclaimed admiringly. 'Now that is going to be your place, honey.' And she sewed a curtain to hang over the aperture so that Nigel could sit enthroned in privacy whenever the need arose.

Frances waited for William to come home to dispose of his braised steak, onions and boiled potatoes.

Aunt Clara had certainly been different. Although she had no children of her own she had been delicious to everybody else's, which was probably why she got eaten.

Aunt Clara was a fat, earthy groundling. Once Frances caught a glimpse of her struggling into her corset in the pink bedroom at the front of the house. Her huge breasts were round and doughy like the bread she kneaded on the kitchen table, warm and as if they were still rising. The bedroom's pink wallpaper had gigantic white flowers on it. Over the windows lacy curtains fell negligently and the sun, though it raged and burned outside, came in very quietly, on tiptoe. Beside the windows hung long pink velvet curtains which gave the room an opulent look. They were reflected in the wardrobe like a cathedral which towered in the hush. The two beds, dark mahogany with polished headboards, shone like deep pools on which white bedspreads floated like water lilies. Between the beds there was just enough room for one person at a time to pass on the goatskin rug. The whole room was in fact not large but its grandeur, like Aunt Clara's, encompassed every detail, from the crystal perfume bottle and the silver hairbrush on the heavy dressing table to the small, embroidered pillow filled with herbs which kept away the croup.

The room in which the children slept was separated from the hallowed place by a beaverboard partition. This was all that there was between Uncle Sam's bed and the bed in which Frances slept. Frances decided very soon after the opening of the curtains after the measles, when they began to observe their new surroundings, that it was a good thing Aunt Clara's bed was close to Uncle Sam's because it made it easier for Aunt Clara and Uncle Sam to get into Uncle Sam's bed together late at night. She had no idea why they got into the same bed but whatever they did they obviously enjoyed it because there was always a lot of laughing and talking. She would lie and hear the poplar leaves in the dark heat outside the house clapping their hands gently in a breath of wind, as though applauding the hugger-mugger of activity and merriment within.

'Holy bald-headed suffering cats,' Uncle Sam said when they showed him the pond they had made and filled with creatures from the creek which ran between the hill and the New Road, which they were forbidden to go anywhere near. This was the most extravagant expression Aunt Clara allowed him to use. When he used it Frances and Nigel always knew that he was impressed.

'Now then, Sam,' Aunt Clara would say. 'We're going to have supper in the garden so start up the fire and I'll bring you out a pan of corn.'

The mosquitoes made electrical noises and swarmed around Aunt Clara as they all sat in the crimson sunset with butter dripping down their chins from the big yellow corn cobs and the little train went hooting westwards from one side of the horizon to the other through the fields, its wailing into the receding light accompanied by joyous song from Toby, Uncle Sam's small black dog. The whole evening was brushed with the scent of Aunt Clara's pink and white peonies which abandoned themselves all over the garden, their heads as big and heavy as dinner plates.

Frances sat in her kitchen waiting for William to come home from work to eat his steak and onions and potatoes.

Cold makes one aware of heat. If Aunt Clara had been her mother, she would never have grown up with the sense of good fortune that she had. If she had not been made to feel useless and a mess she might never have recreated herself in the full enjoyment of the mess she was.

Aunt Clara would have understood about William and Albert.

During the four years that she fostered her niece and nephew she instilled in them, with the utter relaxation born of Scotch, a great love for all mankind.

Frances could hear William tramping up the path. Her heart went out to him. Imagine working hard all day and then coming home to her cooking.

❧

8

Alice wondered what to do. Joan had a problem as well, but hers was less testing.

While they had been drinking coffee and draining off the flood waters, Endymion had painted Martin with emulsion paint which the boys had discovered in Alice's shed. Martin had also painted Endymion. But Martin had painted Endymion with gloss.

'Dymmie darling, aren't you a pretty colour?' said Alice. She surveyed the dripping yellow object which stood before her on the kitchen floor.

'Martin is green,' Endymion explained.

'I see,' said Alice, the dusty sunlight coming through gothic windows in the library of her mind. 'Exactly what happened, my love?'

'Martin and I found the paint in the shed. We painted the shed.'

'And some of the paint got on to you? Accidentally?' Alice was fair to a fault.

'No,' said Endymion reasonably. 'No, Alice, that wasn't what happened. We painted the walls and we painted the garden fork, then we painted all those plant pots and the floor and a few other things. Then there was some paint left so I painted Martin. So he painted me. But there wasn't any more green, so he painted me yellow.'

'Ah,' said Alice. 'He painted you yellow because you ran out of green.' She was close to being perturbed. 'Well, I think we'll have to get some of it off,' she apologised. 'I'll tell you what, petal. You stand there while I go and get some turpentine.'

She rooted gingerly amongst the freshly painted objects in the shed. There were yellow and green garden implements of almost every shape and size but she could find nothing that resembled a bottle of turpentine.

Alice plodded to Joan's back door leaving a pattern of yellow and green footprints on the paving stones. Noticing the footprints and realising that she was ruining the patio she changed her mind and started back towards the road, leaving a double trail behind her.

She walked through the village to the shop noticing that the footprints were becoming fainter.

'Six bottles of turpentine, please, Mr Todd,' she said.

'Going to be busy, my dear,' old Mr Todd replied, lifting the bottles from a low shelf and disappearing down the cellar stairs to look for a box to put them in.

'Painting the kitchen?' he asked as he returned.

'No. It's just Endymion,' said Alice. 'He's yellow.'

'He's yellow,' Mr Todd repeated. Nothing would surprise him about Endymion. When Endymion came into the shop Mr Todd moved round from behind the counter and followed him closely as he explored the vegetables, the pop bottles, the penny sweet box, the crisp packets, the butterfly nets, the crayon books and the racks of folded gift wrappings, happy if the child left with only one major spillage to be put right.

'I'm afraid I'll have to scrub him,' Alice continued dejectedly. 'It would be nicer just to let it wear off. You know, I don't like to discourage them when they are being creative. But it's wet, you see. Everything would get yellow if I didn't.'

'Everything would get yellow.' Mr Todd nodded understandingly.

If Endymion had been his child a few things would have got red from time to time.

While his mother was away Endymion, judging that she had forgotten him, lay down on the brown leather sofa. Then he stood up again. He surveyed the sofa. There was a yellow shadow of his body on it. Dimly, from the far away depths of last winter, he remembered how his mother had demonstrated a good method of making angels. You lay on your back in the snow with your arms wide apart. Then you moved them carefully up and down so that they flattened the snow in a wide arc on each side of your body. This produced wings.

He lay down on the sofa, fitting his body carefully into the shape that was already there. Then he moved his arms up and down and stood up again.

It was amazing. Indelibly fixed on the dark brown leather was a perfect yellow angel, its wings spread as if it were about to embark upon some beatific mission.

When Alice returned with Mr Todd's box full of bottles of turpentine he was still standing there, transfixed.

'An angel,' he announced grandly, enclosing the sofa with a wide sweep of his yellow arm. Some of the paint having come off on the sofa he was dripping less.

'Oh how lovely, flower,' said Alice doubtfully. 'But I think we'll have to try to take some of this nice yellow off before Daddy gets home.'

Endymion was all attention. Mummy was one thing. Daddy was a different kettle of fish. He followed his mother obediently up the two flights of stairs to the bathroom.

Next door Martin had been washed, scolded, put into his pyjamas and made to sit at the table until tea was ready. But Martin had only been painted with emulsion.

'Whatever made you do a stupid thing like that? You know perfectly well paint is for tables and chairs and walls, not for boys,' said Joan.

'We painted the walls as well,' Martin pointed out. 'It was Endymion's idea,' he added grudgingly. Endymion always had the best ideas.

Unaware that there had been a difference in consistency as well as in colour between the yellow and the green paint he did not know that Endymion's plight was worse than his. He stung a little from the vigorous rubbing his mother had given him with soap and water.

But he didn't sting half as much as Endymion stung when Alice, having scraped him with turpentine and the face cloth, turpentine and the nail brush, turpentine and the loofah and turpentine and the pumice stone, on an inspiration put the plug and her son in the bath, gave him a few of Hadrian's ships to play with, emptied the remaining five bottles of turpentine on top of him and left him there to soak.

9

It had been a society wedding, perhaps even the wedding of the year in that small Lancashire town. William's mother and Hermione were determined that there should be no doubt in anybody's mind about their young people having been married.

William's mother knew that he, having been brought up properly, was thoroughly ready for all the responsibilities the state entailed. Hermione knew, in her heart of hearts, that all the expensive education had taught Frances nothing.

Hermione knew that William had been brought up properly, that he was more than conversant with the social graces which Frances lacked and that although he couldn't expect to keep her in the style to which she had been accustomed he would certainly be polite to her and possibly improve her.

William's mother knew that Frances was hopeless. But such a sweet girl. And, of course, well-educated.

Neither of them felt that Frances should be entrusted to decide what sort of a wedding she would like. Such matters were for mothers.

Frances woke up feeling sick. Sunlight gently stirred the new chestnut leaves in the part of the garden which George called his wilderness. Nearer to the house, on his manicured lawn, a marquee stood splendidly flanked by hundreds of imported pot plants which blazed round the stone walls like guardsmen waiting for the queen.

There were to be six bridesmaids. One of them, Dorothy, had spent the night in Celia's old bed. Celia, long married, was unable to be present at her sister's wedding as she was again engaged in reproduction.

'Do you want an aspirin?' Dorothy asked, looking critically at the bride who was standing at the window with her hands pressed against the sides of her head, her pyjama trousers held up by a piece of red wool.

'I'd rather have a head transplant.'

'No time for that. You should have thought of it yesterday.'

'Suppose I pass out before we reach the altar. Hermione will be awfully angry if she has gone to all this trouble and we emerge from the ceremony unmarried.'

'That's what I'm here for. Chief bridesmaid. I shall take your flowers from you and the others will gather discreetly around and gather you to themselves as I repeat your vows in a disguised voice and you will be wed by proxy. If you look as bad then as you do now everybody will be so relieved that it is all over there'll be no questions asked.'

'We aren't really going to be married anyway. William being an atheist and all that.'

'Frances, I don't think this is the time for theological maunderings. Go and wash your face and remove your virginal nightwear. Then let's get you into this wedding gown.'

'Well, I suppose I shall be married. I'm not an atheist. But William won't. I shall just be married to a bachelor.'

'William is the most correct man in England. He knows precisely what he is doing. He won't even drop the ring. He'll certainly be married, if we ever get you to him at the altar.'

Aunt Clara hadn't been able to come from Canada. But Aunt Elizabeth had.

She entered the bedroom at this moment and said to Frances,

'I hope Hermione has told you about things. I mean, you

only have to do it once, you know. Your cousin Hilda had Paul who was planned. But then she had Florence and Ethel and Harry and Jason who weren't.'

Aunt Elizabeth had always come straight to the point. It occurred to Frances that in fact Hermione had not told her about things, ever. Not that it mattered. She offered to show Aunt Elizabeth some of her recent paintings but Dorothy said they could get together on painting after the honeymoon.

'I'll have that aspirin now,' said Frances.

Walking through the churchyard to take his daughter up the aisle of the crowded church George wished that she could have been married in a mission hut. He walked slowly, trying to disengage the sunlight through the gravestones and this strange, serious Frances in the white dress with bridesmaids hovering ahead of them in the arched entrance from his glum anticipation of the bills. As the maidens lined up behind them and Dorothy straightened Frances and her train, the church was a garden of wedding hats and the music began to have its sepulchral effect on them all.

William was standing with his brother Herbert.

Halfway to William, Frances tugged at George's arm.

'Daddy,' she said. 'Thanks for everything, Daddy.'

'We'll talk about that later,' said George, not sure whether if he cried it would be because he was losing Frances or because Hermione was calling everyone My Lord.

Although Hermione felt inferior to nobody, because of her convent upbringing she was always excessively polite to clerics.

And there seemed to be large numbers of them.

Most of them were people whom Frances regarded as dear friends. Most of them were dear friends of George and Hermione. But they all had to be addressed as if they were only one or two down from the Almighty.

As the procession approached, William turned and bowed a deep bow. He led Frances up to the chancel steps, followed by Herbert who looked nervous.

Dorothy and her handmaidens stood clutching their posies. Frances had lost her headache.

Here was William, solid, strong, respectable William. He

was here to represent the Establishment (all except God), the
status quo, bread and butter, security, comfort. As long as
she was with William she would never have to worry about
anything, for William knew just where he was going. He did
his duty and he did it with impeccable sobriety of purpose,
keeping on going, up the steps, past the altar, through the
reredos, out into the churchyard via the stained-glass window
and on into the life to come, except that he didn't believe in
that. Here and now, the pivot of a grand social occasion, he
was in his element.

He just hoped that Frances wouldn't put her foot in it.

Dear Frances. You never knew what Frances would do.

At least she hadn't come up the aisle in her wellingtons.

Frances remembered the lovely holiday she and William
had spent in France the preceding summer. Hermione had
made them travel on separate planes and stay with French
families connected with their own respective families so that
nobody would know they had in fact gone on holiday
together. But William, throwing caution to the winds as
cautious young Englishmen will when they are abroad,
climbed up a fire escape outside the flat in which Frances was
living and Frances had let him in.

She supposed that was the last adventure she and William
would have.

Dear William. She squeezed his arm and he squeezed back,
partly to draw her attention to the fact that they had nearly
reached the bit in the service where she had to speak.

He opened the front door.

'Ah, you've been painting again,' he said amicably.

'Albert and I wanted to get those trees while the sun was on
them.'

'Nice. I like it better than the last one. Any food?'

William put down his briefcase and moved a pile of plates
in the sink so that he could wash his hands.

He always said, 'Any food?' like that. It was his way of
suggesting that if there wasn't, it didn't matter, which he
always felt it was safe to do because there always was some –
food of some kind, anyway – and Frances was very good at

serving it as if she had been slaving over a hot stove all day, as his mother had.

'Notice anything?' she asked.

William looked around the kitchen. It was in its usual state.

'Give me a clue.'

'About me.'

William examined his wife.

'You've had your hair cut,' he exclaimed, as if he had discovered a new planet.

'The Mayor said that I had had my ears lowered.'

'Must ask the Mayor for some horsemuck for the roses.'

'And Howard has left Thelma.'

'Little Howard. Who would have thought it.'

William ate his meal, a look of polite gallantry on his face. Frances fell silent.

It was like being put into a cradle and rocked, having William at home.

'Hermione has been going on about the drains again,' she said.

'It's only the heat.'

'And she wants you to move the wood outside the back door.' Frances grasped the metaphorical spoon and stirred the psychological pudding.

'Like hell I will.' William opened his newspaper and turned to the legal page.

Twenty-eight years later Frances realised that she had been wrong. It was all an adventure with William. William, the devout atheist, William the husband of social order, William the true, the just, the unperturbable had stood beside her at the altar pleased that she had remembered not to come up the aisle in her wellingtons. And such little blessings had kept him going from day to day through nearly three decades.

The little blessings that had kept Frances going were her constant visits to the blue cradle, touching the baby's warm red cheek.

❦

'Just look at that. Will you just look at that?'

Frances and Hermione were standing in the queue at the till in Marks and Spencer's.

It was hot and the shoppers, wearing dresses with low backs and displaying brown shoulders and arms, looked tired and anxious to get home.

In front of Hermione a harassed-looking man with his shirtsleeves rolled up was offering a fifty-pound note to the cashier in payment for his groceries.

'A fifty-pound note,' said Hermione in a voice which drew the attention of all the shoppers within a radius of four tills each way. 'I've never had a fifty-pound note in my life and here's this man paying for his groceries with one. Poor old pensioners like me have to do our best to manage and people like him pay for their groceries with fifty-pound notes.' She was crimson with rage.

'I think you should lower your voice, Mother,' said Frances, acutely conscious of the interest that was being shown in them.

'I will not lower my voice. Things like that should be brought out into the open. There's too much of it going on. People spending money like water. I'd be ashamed. I wouldn't be able to hold my head up.'

By now her victim did indeed look as if he could not hold his head up. Not looking at Hermione, who was fumbling in her shabby leather purse among the coins and the tattered one-pound notes, he addressed himself to the young cashier.

'It's the post office,' he explained humbly. 'They've got a notice up saying they're sorry they have to pay the dole in large notes this week.' He began to pack his shopping into a dilapidated carrier bag, putting the eggs at the bottom in his haste to escape from the dock.

'They've all got more money than they know what to do with. Sit around and don't work. Nobody gives me fifty-pound notes.' Hermione was flying high.

Everyone was now watching them.

'If you don't shut up and mind your own business, Mother, I shall leave you here,' said Frances wishing to disassociate herself from this horrifying scene.

It did, after all, look different if you knew that this inoffensive man was being set upon by someone who had spent most of her life being waited on by servants and driven about in the back of a Rolls Royce.

'Not to worry,' said the cashier cheerfully to her beleaguered customer. 'We've had a few big notes today. No problem.' She gave him an encouraging smile.

'It shouldn't be allowed,' said Hermione to the whole world. 'It just should not be allowed.'

The culprit turned and looked enquiringly at Hermione for the first time as he prepared to lug his shopping home. He shrugged his shoulders at the neat little figure in the blue linen suit bought forty years ago at Kendal Milne's in Manchester and paid for on account by a husband who settled all the bills.

'Altogether too much money about.' Hermione glared at him and he walked away.

This, thought Frances, is the sort of thing that pushes people over the edge. You can go on so far and then you meet somebody like my mother. It reminds you, as if you needed to be reminded, that the world is only there to trample you underfoot.

❦

Alice was thinking about *The Glass Bead Game*. The convolution of thought in it thrilled her. Everything was one. Everything that existed should be seen in the light of everything else . . . She thought with envy of the old Music Master, dying in a state beyond saintliness in an aura of radiance produced by music, meditation, mathematics, discipline and love.

She glanced up from her book to observe Marcus who was reading *The Hobbit*. Marcus had been reading since he was three and a half. By four he had been able to make good sense of the front page of the *Guardian*, within its limits.

Endymion and Hadrian had gone to the swimming baths with Joan and Martin. She had the afternoon to herself. At least, she had the afternoon with Marcus, which amounted to the same thing. Marcus was a joy to be with. Occasionally he consulted her about the meaning of a word, but since she had taught him how to use a dictionary it was more often only ideas that he wanted explained.

If she hadn't met David at Oxford Alice would have stayed on and become a don. She didn't really regret that she hadn't. But she couldn't explain her apparent inadequacy as a housewife and mother in the way that she could explain legends to Marcus, or the working of the seasons to Hadrian and Endymion. She couldn't explain to critical observers that she never thought about the dangers which lie in wait at every turn for healthy boys. She couldn't explain that she never thought about her husband after he had gone off to work, that his arrival home in the late afternoon always gave her a shock of surprise. Joan cleaned and washed and polished and cooked quite happily all day long. Alice couldn't explain that these activities drove her demented. Unless she was reading or writing, her mind, bursting with unconsummated thought, blundered hither and thither crashing blindly into the sides of its enclosure like a maddened bull. She couldn't explain that she had the intelligence to appreciate every aspect of every problem and that this made it as impossible to make even the smallest practical decision as it would be for the bull to associate the pain he was inflicting upon himself with his furious inclination to rush at the walls.

And when she had a practical idea, it invariably ended in an impractical manner.

As a baby Endymion had spent all his nights banging the end of his cot with his head.

In the upstairs living room with David Alice would sigh. 'I suppose it comforts him.'

'Wood against wood,' said her husband. 'He's a punchie.'

'What about the fontanelle? It could be irreversible, the damage.'

'Nothing much to damage in Endymion's head, I shouldn't wonder. But he ruins the music, thundering about like that.'

They heard the familiar rumble of cot wheels as Endymion's labours set it on its nightly stroll across the bedroom floor.

'Perhaps,' said Alice suddenly, 'I mean, perhaps if we could anchor it so it doesn't move, he might stop. It could be the motion of the cot that spurs him on. Echoes of the mother's body while he was in utero. Would it be worth trying? If the cot didn't move, I mean, he might realise that he had been born.'

David went out to the shed and came back with a screwdriver, his drill and four large screws. Climbing up the narrow stairs he entered the boys' bedroom.

A few minutes later Alice heard the shrill squeal of the electric drill and turned up the record player. Both noises failed to wake either the baby or Hadrian, sleeping in his bed by the front window.

David returned with a look of deep satisfaction.

The music soared. He sat down next to his wife on the sofa.

'That'll fix the bugger,' he said.

Alice couldn't believe it. She had been practical. She had solved a problem.

'What did you do?' she asked, putting her arm around David's neck and rubbing his cheek with her nose.

He put his arms around her.

'Two bloody big screws through each leg of the cot into the skirting board,' he replied, stroking her thigh.

The music filled the cottage. From upstairs there was silence.

Alice was getting lost, lost in the permutations of the music, lost in the universal feelings that being close to David roused in her.

She came to with a shock.

A regular thud-thudding had begun again upstairs.

Tears shone in her eyes.

'It didn't work,' she said. 'Why does he do it? What is wrong with him? If it isn't the movement of the cot, what is it? His bones will be flat. He'll have a flat head, like one of those lumpen hammers builders use.'

'Ignore him,' said David, who had begun to think of ways of forgetting about Endymion. He undid Alice's blouse.

The music rose and fell. Alice unzipped David's jeans and put her hand inside the opening.

'I'm sure we should do something about him,' she protested, undoing the top button of his shirt with her other hand and pressing her lips against his neck.

'He has to take his chances like all the rest of us,' said David, no longer paying a lot of attention to the problem.

They fell on to the floor, trying to discard enough clothing quickly enough to deal with the urgent mood which had come upon them.

As the rhythm of their bodies was reaching a crescendo, as Alice, no longer troubled by the conflict between the material and the immaterial worlds, gave vent to female mating cries, as the music from the record player filled their ears and the thudding of Endymion's head against the end of his cot punctuated the upper air, as David prepared to withdraw, as he had with miraculous success since Endymion was born, there came a thunderous noise from the room above. Drowning the uproar of the music, the sounds of David's panting and Alice's little screams of delight it continued, an ominous tearing and splintering, followed by the purposeful rolling of the wheels of the cot on its relentless mission across the floorboards.

David missed his cue and it was several seconds before, disengaging themselves, they sat up on the floor and sorted out what belonged to whom. Finding his jeans David raced up the narrow staircase and flung open the bedroom door. Endymion's cot was parked on the opposite side of the room against Hadrian's bed whence it could proceed no further. Firmly screwed to its two back legs was a six-foot length of skirting board, still quivering with the excitement of its departure from the wall.

Alice appeared in the doorway behind her husband. She was dressed in her bra which hasty application had left with one side of her bosom hanging below the cup, and a cardigan attached around her waist by its sleeves modestly covering her bottom but leaving the rest of her naked.

'Samson,' she murmured, her eyes huge with the aftermath of love and the wonder of creation. 'He must have the strength of Samson.'

David scratched his head.

'It's breast-feeding that does it,' Alice explained, drawing the cardigan together.

'My god,' said David, 'and I didn't get out in time.'

Alice looked fondly at Marcus, his round National Health glasses trained inexorably on *The Hobbit*.

Nature was wonderful.

12

❧

The Mayor mopped his brow. Now that he was forking the hay into his barn he had resorted to wearing trousers again. He could feel the sweat running down his legs. His beard was matted in dark wet strings. The cobblestones of the yard glittered in the sun, pale green and uneven with centuries of wear, dotted with small islands of hay like a grey sea waiting to be discovered in some uncharted region.

He was hot. His face was crimson. His bright blue eyes were glazed, as if he had drawn blinds over them to hide from himself something which he knew it would hurt him to see.

He was not only hot. He was also very angry.

While he had been in the village during the morning, in the course of collecting his ration of rum, or 'diesel' as he liked to call it, he had overheard a conversation between two old ladies which was not meant for his ears. When they became aware of his presence the two old ladies had begun to discuss, in an exaggeratedly loud tone, the terrible price of meat. But he had been informed, brutally and crudely, that his brother-in-law had run off with some loose piece from the town who worked as a secretary in the same department of the council.

'Farting git. Runt. Son of a duck egg.'

He had been describing Howard to himself all afternoon and the exercise which his body was engaged in, combined with the intense heat and this verbal workout, had driven him to a point of exhausted fusion at which he had become highly combustible.

Thelma had been more like his child than his sister. He felt all the rage and indignation that a father feels, thinking of her abandoned by that rat. She was alone. She was the subject of gossip in the village. Howard had done this to her.

The Mayor had been twenty when his sister was born. She came as something of a surprise, Agnes their mother being forty-two and Jeremiah, their father, sixty and crippled with arthritis. Already Jeremiah had handed over most of the responsibility for the running of the farm to his young son and the Mayor had shouldered it with blunt good humour.

Agnes had wrapped the red little baby in a knitted blanket and put her in front of the fire in a drawer taken from the sideboard and emptied – the Mayor's cradle having long gone to Jeremiah's brother's family who had seemed to fill cradles with the regularity of Jeremiah's sheep. The Mayor had been torn between his love for this infant and the embarrassment that her birth caused.

After her christening at the Chapel he had been subjected to an agony of leg-pulling by the other farmers' sons who would not have dared to say to Jeremiah or their own fathers what they said to him.

'Plainly not his but thine. Who's given it thy mother from thee. Wore it young Kate Armistead? She been a bit plump lately.'

The Mayor had only had one love in his life. When she turned him down and married the son of one of the mill-owners he had turned his back on matrimony and devoted himself to looking after the farm and his ailing father, and now he intended to take on this unexpected sister.

But he never forgot his intended. She had not been particularly pretty, not for instance as pretty as little Thelma turned out to be, but she had been particularly well-endowed about the bust. The Mayor, since his childhood, had noticed women's busts. As he grew older he became obsessed with the power of the breast.

Passing through the village to collect his diesel or his groceries he would call out to the young women wheeling prams from the new estate,

'It's breast-feeding that does it. It's the colostrum. Pep up thy paps and yon babby will never look back.'

If he could persuade one of them to stop and listen to him he would explain that it was just the same with humans as it was with lambs.

'Now the mother sheep can tell which is her lamb by the smell of the colostrum. If she nuzzles a lamb's bum she can tell by smell which one is passing her colostrum,' he would say.

When Jeremiah died at seventy, bent as a black hawthorn twig, so gnarled was he by his disease that the undertakers had to squash his body in order to be able to close the lid of the coffin. It had always grieved the Mayor, the memory of his gentle old father being nailed down forcibly. He had been such a docile and kindly man. Perhaps the spirit which had kept him moving painfully about his farm for the last twenty years had still been trying to keep him above the earth he loved.

Agnes died at eighty, having been in good health until she had a fall while feeding her hens. It was when he no longer had Agnes to consider and little Thelma was taken care of — happy, as it seemed, with her Howard and their two children, though Howard had always seemed to him to be a pillock — that the Mayor had finally allowed his predilection for rum to become his support and mainstay.

'Couple of pints of diesel, Mr Todd,' he would say with a wink, and Mr Todd would give him half a tumbler free out of the barrel to try, as in the best wineshops.

'Aye, that'll do, thank you kindly,' the Mayor would say, draining the tumbler and replacing it on the counter.

Then Mr Todd would fill the Mayor's bottles and he would go on his way, in tune with whatever season they were in, warmed in the snow, refreshed in the sun, cheered in the isolation of the ancient farmhouse, with its few acres of land and its comfortable beasts, all known by name.

And now the little creep had left her. Left his sister Thelma for a platinum blonde dolly. If he had been a rat, an actual rat, the Mayor would have got him straight through the tail end, where he needed it, the Mayor thought with satisfaction. He spat out a piece of hay which had lodged in his mouth and felt scorched with indignation.

Of course, Thelma hadn't told him. His Thelma wouldn't tell him a thing like that. She was a proud lass. She had always been a proud lass, and loyal to that bastard, heaven knows why. He had heard other bits of conversation not meant for his ears before this morning. Why she had married that pipsqueak from the council offices and gone to live in a box on the new estate he would never know. There had been many an honest farmer's son would have been filled with satisfaction to have her mending in front of his fire, feeding the weak lambs with a bottle and seeing to a couple of kiddies.

Agnes, though, had always seemed to think there was something fine about Thelma's married state. She had walked proudly down the lane once a week to the polished chrome set-up that called itself a house in which her daughter lived, carrying apple jelly made from the apples of the patient old trees of the farm, or gooseberry jam or blackberry pie to please her grandchildren, Karen and Andrew.

You couldn't trust townspeople. They didn't know about things. There was Thelma, younger than her mother had been when she was born, left on her own because her husband, if you could call him that, had grown tired of her. There was no justice in it. No justice and no sense.

He ought to shoot the little shit. He would, by god, he would. He'd find out where he'd gone and let him know that if he thought so little of Thelma there were others who thought more of her.

He heard his mother's voice, her mouth pursed in a warning shape, saying,

'Act in haste, repent at leisure.'

'If I knew where the devil was I'd get him,' he replied to the shade of Agnes, and left the farmyard, passing his mother's little walled garden in which the roses and blue geraniums, let go since her death, were having a drunken orgy, throwing themselves, entangled and riotous, over the paths; the roses drenched with perfume, the geraniums bluer and more intense than the solid sky.

He left his boots at the door and padded down the flagged passage followed by Sarah the old sheepdog who was fit for nothing but lying in the sun these days but always got up to greet him when he appeared.

He stood by the window of the kitchen. The day's exercise which had drawn some of the hatred from his breast was over and he could feel the anger growing inside him like a bad attack of indigestion.

'By god, if I knew where he was, I'd blast his head off,' he said to Flora the cat who was about to become a mother again, looking out of the window at a row of six dead rats which he had lined up on the stone wall.

'Dead as a rat,' he added.

He drank a refreshing tumblerful of diesel oil and a vision of his sister Thelma sitting sobbing in her plastic cage surrounded by her two sobbing children roused him to a rare state of fury.

He took his gun from the wall of the passage, struggled back into his boots and made off unsteadily down the lane.

13

In the long mirror on the outside of her wardrobe door Hermione could see the pink cotton dress. It had straps over the shoulders and showed her bare arms and back, brown and freckled from the hot sun.

'Not bad,' she said to herself. 'I'm not bad for seventy-two.'

Her white hair shone, waved at the front and drawn back in a tidy twist at the base of her neck. The dress showed her figure to good advantage.

She wasn't so sure about her face. She approached the

mirror and examined herself. This reminded her of Snow White.

'Mirror, mirror on the wall, who is the fairest of us all?' she asked her reflection, and added with a resigned sigh, 'Not me, anyway.'

Her nose was becoming like dear Clara's, large and luminous. Of course, it had caught the sun, but there was no denying it. Only Elizabeth of the three sisters had escaped their father's nose. Clara used to say that she kept her brains in hers.

'Momma,' thought Hermione, turning to look at the sepia photograph of the mother she could barely remember, 'Momma had a beautiful nose.'

Now they were all dead, Poppa, Elizabeth and Clara as well as poor Momma. The only living souls who remembered her as she had been when she was a child were Freda and one or two other girls with whom she had been at school and she didn't hear from them often.

Freda had been big as a girl.

They were supposed to be translating Latin unseens. Sister Mary had slipped out for a few moments, exhorting them to be quiet and diligent in her absence.

'Let's do something,' Freda had said.

'We are doing something,' Susanne replied, glumly surveying the pages of *Caesar's Gallic Wars*.

'No, I mean something bad,' Freda went on.

'God will strike you down,' Jacquie had said, using her ruler as a sword to demonstrate the act. It flew out of her hand and landed on the floor at the front of the room.

The others stopped struggling with the unknown.

'She'll be back any minute,' Hermione warned.

'What can we have fun with?' Jacquie asked despondently. They were in the Music Room. 'There's nothing in here to have fun with.'

'Let's push the piano in front of the door,' Freda suggested.

Not far below the level at which piety drifts, its white wings gently paddling through the soft air of heaven, a red hot cockatoo shuffles up and down on his branch uttering obscenities.

The fifteen twelve-year-olds in their ugly black tunics with high collars, tired of the enforced stillness and silence, bored with the intricacies of Latin, decided with the firmness and resolution of a cloud changing shape in a strong wind that pushing the piano in front of the door was just what had been missing from their lives.

They fell upon the magisterial-looking piano with its ornate candle-holders and its upright fretted music stand. The Music Room had a parquet floor and in response to the massed weight of girls, their healthy appetites satisfied mostly by starch products, the piano took to its wheels with abandon, possibly, like them, desirous of raising its Victorian skirts. It glided smoothly towards the door gaining speed as it went.

As it approached the last table its right back wheel, which was at the front as it was moving backwards, struck Jacquie's ruler. This obstacle deflected its course and it veered sharply to the left. The girls, pushing as hard as they could, were unable to right it or steer it back on to its old path. It then struck the edge of the shallow platform designed to raise the nun in charge of the music class high enough above her pupils to command their attention.

With a loud jangling and splintering sound it crashed into the platform and toppled majestically on to its back where it rested with its wheels still revolving squeakily. The girls lay in piles across its yellowed ivory keyboard which was now in a vertical position.

'That's done it,' observed Hermione, rubbing her pelvis which had come sharply in contact with one of the polished brass pedals.

'Perhaps it wasn't such a good idea,' Jacquie added.

The army of movers rubbed themselves in whichever part they hurt and stood thoughtfully surveying the dead piano.

'Well, we'd better get it back before Fairy Mary arrives,' said Freda sensibly, at length.

How to get it back was another problem.

Hermione exchanged a little laugh with her reflection in the wardrobe mirror.

'They all think I'm old and bad-tempered,' she said to it. 'Well, I am.'

She climbed painfully down the carpeted stairs of her cottage and made preparations for her daily walk.

She hung her front door key on its piece of string around her neck and picked up the large grey polythene dustbin liner it was her habit to fill with rubbish as she went on her round of the village.

Outside her front door the sun struck her like a clumsy lover. Her head under its heavy knob of hair began to sweat.

It was a matter of honour to walk the whole length of the hill up to the crossroads where she always allowed herself to sit on the bench, her rubbish in the long grass beside her among the dandelions while she caught her breath.

'None of them has a sense of discipline nowadays,' she told a sparrow which was rolling in the dust beside the road. 'They don't make themselves do things any more.' She gazed at the blue shape of Pendle Hill down in the valley and breathed deeply, leaning back on the bench. 'No sense of duty. No self-control,' she added, forgetting the piano.

Looking like a pink daisy she sat and thought about her daughter Frances. As always thinking about Frances roused a sense of frustration and annoyance. She had made great personal sacrifices to ensure that her children were well brought-up. She had wanted them to make the best of themselves. And what had they done? Other people's children became doctors and lawyers and headmasters. What had hers done? Nothing. Unless you counted getting away from her as fast as they could doing something. They didn't appear to appreciate her at all. Celia and Keith were on the other side of the world where she could not assist them except by writing long admonitory letters, which she did with great pleasure. Nigel, of course, was like her. He managed his life very well and was a blessing. But Frances was hopeless. She simply had no respect for her mother's experience.

Still, it was fortunate that she had been able to come and live next door to Frances when George died and the family home was sold.

There was still time to make something of Frances. It was just a question of getting through to her.

What she must do, somehow, was explain to Frances that entertaining people all day long in her kitchen and painting pictures with strange men and mooching about junk shops and flea markets was not a proper way to spend her life.

She made a mental note to go in and have a word with her daughter when she had finished her walk.

As she stood up and lifted her swag-bag with its treasure of coke tins, empty cigarette cartons, crisp packets and beer bottles, feeding into its mouth a Mars Bar wrapper which had escaped her notice under the seat, she became aware of a figure further up the road.

It was heading towards her in an erratic manner, very red in the face and looking like a grizzly bear being followed by a swarm of hornets. And it was carrying a gun.

14

Contrary to her brother's febrile apprehensions Thelma was not sitting sobbing in her modern box on the new housing estate. Nor were her two children sitting at her knee grieving for their absent father.

At least, none of them was grieving in a visible or audible way. What was going on inside each of them might have been more difficult to determine.

Thelma, like Agnes practical and resourceful and like Jeremiah good-natured, wise and forgiving, was finding jobs to do. She had cleaned the house from top to bottom as if thereby in some way exorcising the evil spirit which had descended upon it.

The children were engaged in preparing for a circus. During school holidays there was always entertainment in the village of Medwell. In the town crowds of bored children looked for mischief. But here there would be a cricket match on the playing field, a trip to the stream with bathing gear and sandwiches and, probably, some exotic scheme for raising money to feed orphans in parts of the world where life was less idyllic or to save ageing animals ruthlessly rejected by people who, unlike these country youngsters, did not feel that animals were exactly like themselves only better. These schemes seemed to grow in the communal child mind like a giant mushroom.

'Mum,' said Andrew, who had not bothered to consider whether being part of a one-parent family was going to alter his life in any way, 'we're having a circus for Blue Peter. Have you got any ringmaster's clothes?'

Thelma marvelled at the confidence with which they asked for the most outlandish things.

'And a fairy dress. I'm riding Blossom,' Karen added.

Blossom was Mr Todd's elderly pony. Blossom was really past being a circus performer, having retired when Mr Todd's children grew up and left home long ago. But she was an old trouper. When she was needed she took part uncomplainingly.

Thelma pulled down the loft ladder and climbing up rummaged in an assortment of boxes under the eaves. Amongst the finery saved after the death of Agnes and Jeremiah she found a bowler hat and some riding breeches, several long dresses of indeterminate age and a flat brown paper parcel tied with hairy, rope-like string which when she opened it disclosed her own wedding dress on top of which was a single rose, faded to the colour of an old suede glove and brittle as thistledown. As she picked it up the rose disintegrated.

'Just like the marriage,' Thelma thought. She put the pieces of the rose on top of the pile of circus clothes, or rather, clothes which might be considered suitable for circus clothes, and climbed back down the ladder.

She had been pregnant. Howard wasn't a big man. But he had a way with him. When she confessed to her mother, Agnes had said,

'Never mind. You were going to get married anyway so there's no harm done. Only next time, tell him to drop his coals outside the door.'

Agnes had been an understanding woman, not vindictive like so many of the good chapelgoers. In response to gossip about couples who were living over the brush she would say,

'Leave them alone. They're not doing anybody any harm. It's their own tools they're using.'

Thelma wished that Agnes had been here now. She would have tried to see Howard's point of view, just as Thelma was trying to see Howard's point of view. But she would also have provided love and reassurance. You didn't realise how much people meant to you until they had gone. On the other hand it would have saddened her mother so much; perhaps it was a good thing that she wasn't here to witness the fall of this establishment which she regarded as being a step higher up in the order of things than the farmhouse.

Andrew and Karen fell upon the clothing and carried it, piled high in front of them, down the road towards the playing field which was seething with children of all shapes and sizes. Blossom, tied to the railings, was eating as much of the long grass round its edges as she could reach, sure in her wise old mind that she was in for a trying afternoon.

'What time does it start?' Thelma called out after them, half wishing that they would come back and ask her for something else.

'We don't know yet. We still have to rehearse,' Karen shouted back over her shoulder. 'We'll let you know. Don't go out.'

'I'll be somewhere around. Maybe at Joan's.' Thelma's voice dwindled into the distance among the chestnut leaves where the trees hung across the road.

As they disappeared Thelma went indoors. It was cool inside, but not as cool as it was during the summer in the farm kitchen with its flagged floor and its thick stone walls.

She felt a great sadness pouring into her. It was like the milk running into the big churns.

This house was not really home. She had not noticed it when Howard was there. Oh yes, there was the three-piece suite, the stainless-steel tea service, the brightly patterned carpet in the sitting room. There was the matching avocado bathroom set (Howard had thought that avocado was a good choice, though she had always thought that pink would have been nicer) and the automatic washing machine and the fawn patterned tiles behind the cooker.

But without Howard these things did not seem precious.

She thought of the stone sink at the farm. She thought of the winking and popping and glistening soap bubbles in the big dolly tub, the brass-headed posser shaped like a conical colander through which the soapy bubbles escaped in grey streams with a sucking sound like that of a thirsty baby when Agnes, her strong brown arms channelled with muscles, pummelled it up and down on wash days. She thought of the crenellated rubbing-board on which her mother had scrubbed the sheets until they shone thin and blue-white across its ridges.

Her brother was right. Some things, though they look bright, are not as valuable as others.

She was not one for living in her memory. What had gone had gone. She had put the farm behind her when she married and, though it had not been let go without sadness, it had gone. Now the allure of this home had gone too.

'We'll build an extension at the back,' Howard had said. 'Like the ones in the magazines. Have two loungers and a few plants out there. Sit in the sun.' But he hadn't done it.

There would be no extension now.

Looking round at her life Thelma thought that there wasn't a lot to show for all the excitement.

Because Howard had been exciting.

Each day of the nine years they had been together had brought some new idea for improving their lot, for boosting themselves up the social ladder.

When you came to think about it, maybe Howard, coming

from the joyless black terraces of the town, had felt that he needed to go up in the world. But what had been wrong with her life, the hens brilliant and confident poking their way around the farmyard, the warm sloppiness of the cows, the spare disarray of the sheep. That was really all you could want from life, if you didn't have somebody like Howard to persuade you otherwise.

She supposed it must have been her fault. She supposed she had never really been his type. He liked girls with make-up who showed their legs and wore pretty clothes and enjoyed dancing. Perhaps his passionate need to make their home as glamorous as possible had been just a substitute for the romantic appeal that she lacked.

Sometimes she had wished that he would talk to her more. He didn't seem to associate making love, for instance, with anything to do with herself. It was something that came over him in an impersonal way. She had never really felt that he was making love to her. He just made love. And in a way, it wasn't really making love, not as she sometimes imagined it, though she had no other experience to compare it with. It was as if by his method of making love Howard had been taking something which it wasn't in him to believe that anyone would actually give him. Thelma would have given him anything.

No good thinking about that.

Howard had gone.

Looking round her home dusted and sparkling on all its surfaces with polish sprayed out of a tin and finding nothing not attended to she decided to go and visit Joan. She would stop at Mr Todd's to buy something for tea. She still had some of the money given to her by Frances. Perhaps if she talked to Joan a way forward would show itself. And she could view the circus as she passed the playing field.

But as she walked slowly down the lane she had a thought which made her walk more slowly for a few moments and then more quickly. She realised that Howard was a clever person who was not real. He knew more facts than she did. He had a better idea of what other people wanted than she did. Yet all the time that she had known him, while he was pretending to help her to know the world he had been secretly taking from her not what she had to give, which she gave anyway, not what a person is entitled to take from a husband or a wife or a friend but what they are not. She realised that Howard had taken her truth, her being, and used it to make himself more attractive to the people he wanted to seem attractive to.

And even as she realised this she knew that she was glad he had gone. She did not want to feed people who wanted to be something that they were not and could only achieve it by stealing from people who trusted them.

15

William was listening to the news as he made his breakfast.

Frances was always fast asleep when he got up. For the first ten or twelve years of their marriage he had tried to waken her.

He felt most alive in the morning. He would have liked her company then. He would have enjoyed telling her something of yesterday's triumphs at the office, relating to her the details of meetings he was to attend today, discussing his plans for improving the services offered by his profession.

All these things she would gladly have listened to in the evening, when she felt at her best. But he was always tired then.

They were like Jack Sprat who could eat no fat and his wife who could eat no lean.

During their lifetime together they had reached a kind of equilibrium. It was the equilibrium that the juggler's saucer has, spinning evenly at the top of its pole, as long as it is kept going fast enough.

He no longer tried to waken her in the morning. She had ceased to try to rouse him to converse in the evening.

At the weekend, in the middle of the day, when Frances was beginning to come alive and he had not yet started to flag they would exchange the week's news. This was their equilibrium. As long as nothing jogged the juggler's arm all was well.

William mashed up a banana and stirred it into his muesli, adding some bran from a cellophane packet. When he was tempted to remember the bacon and eggs, kidneys or kedgeree which had begun his days before he was married, he thought philosophically that this was probably a healthier breakfast for a man of his age in any case.

The news was not good. But was it ever? William was philosophical about bad news as well. He had become attuned to disaster; working with it constantly on a small scale he was not so dismayed by its larger manifestations. Frances was different. She had a horror of tragedy. Tragedy for Frances was being eight years old with your brother and sister on a ship in the middle of the ocean with no adult whom you knew well, surrounded by U-boats which were trying to sink you while you were being carried further and further from the home that you loved towards an unknown future.

William could not explain to her that people who are used to coping with disaster were not driven into a frenzy by it. He could not make her see that for some people organising other people's lives was more important than accepting life's abundant offerings and pushing out of sight any foreboding of ill, as the sailors had made jokes to cover the children's fear, and possibly their own.

She had told him about the red lights.

During lifeboat drill they had been required to test the little red lights which were attached to their lifejackets.

'Tell your brother that if he doesn't stop playing with his it won't be working when we're torpedoed. We won't be able to find him in the water,' a cheerful tar had advised Celia one day when they stood in their long miserable rows. The children had come from all over England and they were blue with cold, paralysed with fear and sick from the endless heaving of the ocean.

William put his plate and his coffee cup into the sink and went upstairs to say goodbye to his wife.

She was lying curled up on her side of the bed, a peaceful expression on her face, her mouth wide open. She always slept with her mouth wide open, as if to allow the words out easily should she wish to reply if anyone spoke unexpectedly.

He looked down at her for a moment. He did not feel envious that she was still asleep. He did not mind that she had nothing pressing to do with her day when it eventually started. He did not think it unfair that he should have to rise early and go off to earn a living for this indolent creature. He bore no grudges. His day would offer him his kind of excitement. Hers would offer her hers.

He bent down and kissed her cheek.

Out poured the words. They were always the same.

'Good heavens. Is it eight o'clock already? I must get up. Oh dear, you've had to make your own breakfast . . .'

He knew that when he had gone she would go back to sleep for another hour. By eleven o'clock she would be more or less human. By the afternoon she would have thought of something nice to do.

By the time she was properly awake he would have done significant things in the real world. It gave him a curious feeling of comfort to know that his wife would be tending an imaginary garden in her imaginary landscape while he worked.

'I'll be back the day after tomorrow,' he said.

'Oh yes. It's the conference. And I didn't even get up to see you off,' she replied, apparently wide awake. He knew that she would be asleep again before he reached the foot of the stairs.

'Well, take care,' she added.

'And you. I'll phone you tomorrow night.'

William walked downstairs with a happy sense of urgency. He mustn't be late at the office. He had a lot to do before

driving to the conference. And when he arrived there he
would see many old colleagues. There would be much to
discuss. He always enjoyed a conference. He knew that
Frances would not miss him. He certainly would not miss
her. There was too much to do. And Frances would be seeing
Albert, checking up on Hermione and drinking tea with her
friends in the village. She might even do another painting.

William liked his wife's paintings. They were like his wife,
not strictly in touch with reality but somehow strangely
reminiscent of it in a way that more functional organisms
often were not.

16

As the figure approached, Hermione realised that it was the
Mayor. He didn't look at all well, very flushed. Of course, it
was hot.

'Good afternoon, Your Worship,' she said with a deferen-
tial smile.

Mayors were more or less in the same category as clergy-
men.

The Mayor drew up sharply and looked at her carefully to
see if she was taking the piss out of him. His eyes moved from
side to side in an effort to focus on the pink person standing
by the bench. He recognised her. It was that Mrs Tattersall,
mother of Frances, who had come to live in the village a
couple of years ago.

No, she wouldn't be pulling his leg. Very polite, Mrs
Tattersall, he had heard, though he had never spoken to her
before. Searching in his usually optimistic soul for anything

that might brighten his black mood he noticed that Mrs Tattersall had an exceedingly well-developed set of breasts.

'Well, as a matter of fact,' he confided, resting his gun on the bench and bending down so that he was closer to these admirable objects, 'I'm not really the Mayor. It's just that they call me that.' Unusually fine. Resplendent and floribundant. Not many of them to the pound.

'Oh, I see.' Hermione was quite unflustered. She could have done without the gun, though.

'Name's Fred. Frederick Holden Pickles. Keep it for the rats,' he added, drawing his gaze reluctantly from Hermione's chest and following her uneasy eyes to his gun. 'Though, as a matter of fact, when I set off I had in mind to use it for other purposes.'

'Holden is an interesting second name,' said Hermione, aware that the Mayor was looking at her in a very personal way and searching for a well-bred gambit to distract his attention.

'Mother's maiden name. Lot of them about. Lot of Pickles, too,' he said.

'Yes, there are a lot of Tattersalls,' she conceded. 'But we come from a very old branch of the family, my husband did, I mean.' Hermione found herself roused by the Mayor's masculinity, his obvious interest in her appearance, and the gun that he was not out to shoot rats with. Though she did wonder whether he could have hit anything in this mood. He seemed to be having difficulty in seeing clearly. 'Rabbits?' she enquired.

'Something nearer to the rat family, but human,' the Mayor said darkly and explained his mission.

Hermione sat down again, cautiously touching the barrel of the gun to make room for herself on the bench.

The Mayor hurriedly slid it along the flaking painted woodwork and deposited it in the grass. Once he had begun to tell his story he felt better. Here was a lady, a real lady, someone in whom a chap could confide. He knew that she was not going to return to the village to toss his predicament about hand to hand like a fairground balloon.

They sat side by side in the sunshine. Beside the Mayor lay

his gun. Beside Hermione her bag of rubbish languished. At their feet the sparrow went about the serious business of its sauna in the dust.

'Now I'm no prude,' the Mayor concluded, 'but it seems a shocking state of affairs to me when a fellow can walk out on a lass like our Thelma who bakes and cleans and mends and looks after him like a king. Some women won't bother, you know. All slack set-up and lackadaisical.'

'I know,' Hermione agreed, thinking of Frances.

'You're a sensible lady,' the Mayor continued after a pause, 'so I'll tell you straight. When I set off from home half an hour ago I was going to blast away at him and string him along the wall with the others.'

Hermione looked thoughtful. She did not know what others the Mayor was alluding to.

'I don't think that would solve the problem,' she said.

The Mayor glanced at her sideways. His vision was clearing. He noticed her sunburned shoulders in the pink dress, her clear, lined face, her neat white hair. His eyes rested on her bosom, gently rising and falling like hills of clover.

He did not know that although she had the nose and Elizabeth hadn't, all three of them were bequeathed the bosom by that sad, faded Momma.

He rejoiced in what he saw, not knowing that he was celebrating a family trait.

I'll bet her childer weren't fed with a homogenised bottle. Plenty of colostrum for them, he thought appreciatively. He made a mental note to observe Frances more closely the next time he saw her. You could always tell when folks had been breast-fed. They had an air about them.

'No,' he replied, 'it wouldn't solve nothing. It would only cause confusion.'

'Violence breeds violence,' said Hermione piously.

'Aye. Too much of it about.'

'Better to make sure that your sister is looked after.'

'She'll come back and live with me, if I can get her out of that box.'

'Where do you live, Your Worship?'

'Fred.'

'Where do you live, Mr . . . er . . . Pickles?'

'Up at Yardale Farm.' The Mayor turned Hermione's head carefully with his big hand, pointing with the other in such a way that he managed to get his arm along the back of the bench behind her.

Hermione was delighted.

'You don't,' she exclaimed. 'You don't really live up there, do you?' She gazed at the roof of the ancient farmhouse which sagged in a hollow between the hills like the shoulders of a tired old man. 'I've seen it on my walks and admired it. I believe there is a part that was built in the sixteenth century.'

'That's right.' The Mayor beamed. 'Falling down, too. Still got the original timbers in the barn.' He edged his arm along so that he could feel the warm flesh at the back of Hermione's neck with his forearm.

He was on to a good thing here.

'Do you see it, the top of the barn between the trees. Historical Society interested in it. What they call a scheduled building.'

It was a long time since he had been so close to a woman.

Hermione, gazing at the distant barn roof, felt his arm against the back of her neck.

'How wonderful,' she said.

It was a long time since she had been so close to a man.

The sparrow, realising that nobody was about to make any sudden movement, called its friends who were hovering near by. They dropped into the dust one by one like the first heavy drops of rain before a thunderstorm. There was a little burst of twittering and fluttering. Then they settled down to rolling and showering each other with the fine, powdery soil.

'Do you come here often?' asked the Mayor at length.

Hermione stopped gazing at the almost derelict barn and pulled herself together.

'Oh, every day. I find I feel a lot better if I have my walk,' she explained. 'I'm seventy-two, you know.' She straightened her skirt with a complacent look on her face.

'Never. Not a day over sixty, like me, I'd have said,' replied the Mayor with some sincerity. Obviously a lady who not only had the right ideas but kept well, too. Preserved, mellow and ripe like a good plum.

'I was born in Canada, you see. Life was much tougher there than it is here.'

'Lot of snow there in the winter. In the winter they get a lot of snow in Canada, so I believe,' the Mayor encouraged her.

Hermione told him about her childhood. She told him about skating on the ponds, the way the ice would bend under your weight in the spring when the thaw began and you had to keep moving or you would go through it, she told him about the maple trees and gathering the maple syrup which was boiled in big metal pots and spread on the snow to cool and harden. She told him about summer camp in the Laurentian Mountains where they slept in log huts and learned some of the skills of the Indians and swam in the warm lake under the white stars and the sky was black as the pupil of your eye when the counsellors thought they were asleep. She told him about her mother's death when she was five, about being brought up by Clara and Elizabeth, about her dear old father who went off to Alaska and had adventures in saloon bars.

The sun had moved some way.

Not feeling any need for a pull at the diesel bottle in his pocket the Mayor was enjoying himself. This was a person of sensibility. This was a person of experience. This wasn't one of your flighty women.

His anger had drifted away into the dandelion-filled meadow behind him, floating from his soul like the seeds of the dandelion clocks.

This was the sort of lady who understood the importance of the breast.

He wouldn't bring the subject up just now. First meetings had to be managed gently, like a shy young horse. But he knew in his deepest recesses that there was an hour or two's good conversation waiting for him in the not too far-off future.

❧

17

Howard lay on the bed in Sharon's flat.

It was a miserable flat and he was feeling miserable. If he had known, he would have thought about the move for more than the week that it had occupied his thoughts.

The flat was next door to a furniture shop. The furniture in the furniture shop was very tasteful – green and gold Dralon-covered suites and modern mahogany standard lamps with elegant tasselled shades. There were also solid, respectable-looking pouffes, stools with fur tops, dinner wagons with raised edges, and gilt and onyx table lamps.

When he was returning from the Town Hall each day Howard stopped and spent a few minutes appreciating these articles of furniture. For him they spelled success, success and prestige.

Underneath the flat was a betting shop. During business hours you could hear the roar of the races and the laughter and conversation of the bookies' clients.

Looking into the window of the furniture shop before he put his key in the lock of the flimsy door with its doorbell hanging out like a dislocated eyeball and mounted the shabby staircase which led to the flat helped to anaesthetise the pain which he suffered as he entered the dark corridor from which the bed-sitter, the bathroom and the kitchenette of his beloved's home slunk furtively like people hoping to pass unnoticed.

The bathroom was black and white, or rather, the washbasin and the lavatory were black and white. The bath was black and gritty yellow. The single cupboard in the kitchenette was pale blue with yellow around its panels and the gas water heater, which leaned at an angle, emitted a constant smell of gas.

In the bed-sitting room languished the double bed with its soiled headboard which must once have been sky-blue satin to match the bedspread which was still sky-blue satin, but only in parts. There presided over this room a huge ugly wardrobe built in the nineteen-thirties which looked as if it had been the resting place of generations of shifty garments and an equally unprepossessing dressing table with a mirror in three sections, one section of which had fallen off its hinges. There was also a sofa which smelled of feet and an armchair richly patterned with cigarette burns. A card table with two chairs lacking backs completed the décor of Howard's love-nest, except for a gas fire attached to the wall by a series of pipes, all bent and downtrodden and hissing as if in response to the leaks from the kitchenette.

Howard had intended to put all this right when he first entered Sharon's home as a new bridegroom but his enthusiasm, two weeks later, had been suffocated by the reproaches of these objects.

He lay on the bed and thought in a resigned and hopeless way that it was criminal to charge twenty-five pounds a week rent for such a penthouse. He gazed at the walls, a uniform coffee colour, once white but thus transformed by the smoke from many thousands of cigarettes and the fumes from the two gas monsters. The floor was covered by linoleum with red, green and yellow squares on it, and a piece of paper-thin brown carpet from which the pile had balded lay despondently at its centre.

Howard thought about his avocado bathroom suite.

Had he made a wise move?

Sharon had such a magical way with her. Sleeping with Sharon was like finding a whole new landscape, a landscape in which the housing estate of his dreams stretched out towards eternity, endless rows of tidy, shining lives with all mod cons, and all arranged by him.

He knew that part of her attraction for him lay in the fact that he was senior to her in the office. He knew that she had enjoyed many lovers before he came within her grasp. He was also shrewd enough to know that one of Sharon's pleasures consisted of bringing down established edifices. Before he had fallen for her charms he had heard other men at the office commiserating with each other in the midst of their ruins. But he had thought that with him it would be different. He hadn't anticipated that he would miss Thelma and the children. He hadn't realised that a constant supply of instant sex did not make up for the absence of patterned tiles behind the cooker and a nice three-piece suite.

Lying waiting for Sharon to come back from the fish and chip shop with their tea he even allowed himself a moment's nostalgia for Thelma's steak and kidney pudding, her farm fruit cake and her scones.

Love, if it is to be as great as we demand that it should be, needs to be nourished with love.

Of course, Thelma would manage without him. But it had all come upon him so suddenly, his decision to leave home with Sharon that he had not considered Thelma and Karen and Andrew at all, other than to assure himself that her brother would look after them until he sorted things out legally.

Lying on Sharon's opulent bedspread he decided that he must go and visit his wife, just to make sure that she had enough money, and to make a few arrangements.

He leaped up as he heard the insecure lock being manipulated on the outer door and Sharon's childish voice calling, 'Howie, hello Howie, I'm back.'

Howard hurried to the kitchenette and took two stained knives and forks from the drawer. He arranged them on the card table. There wasn't a tablecloth in the place.

Sharon click clicked along the dark narrow corridor and burst into the bed-sitting room.

'Got you a surprise. Curried chips. Thought it'd be a change,' she announced proudly.

The difference between her way of feeding a man and the method adopted by Frances was that Sharon didn't realise that to be convincing about the trouble you have taken to produce this food you must present it as if in the finest hotel.

'Plates,' she said, 'oh, n'er mind. We can eat out of the

containers. They're nice, these containers, aren't they?'

Howard had not yet had the opportunity to tell Sharon about his stomach. The smell of curry sauce had warned it that it was in for a bad time and it had already begun to complain.

He sat down and began to scrape as much of it off the chips as he could without attracting Sharon's attention.

He had made a decision.

'What are you doing, Howard?' asked Sharon.

He looked stricken.

'It's just that curry doesn't agree with me,' he apologised.

'Then why the hell didn't you tell me? It's much more expensive with curry. Here, don't waste it. Give it to me. I'll eat it.'

'You didn't say you were going to get curry,' Howard pointed out, his voice feeble as the last movements of a butterfly coming out of the attic in the middle of winter.

In times gone by, watching Sharon as she flitted about the office in a long-sleeved blouse with frilly cuffs and a skirt which was just long enough to hide what wasn't too attractive and just short enough to display what was, her blonde hair shining like a shampoo advertisement and her make-up meticulous as that of a Japanese tea-girl, he had envisaged her in just the sort of setting suggested by the window of the furniture shop next door.

He supposed that some women must get themselves done up for work and not bother about their home life.

He would go and make his arrangements with Thelma. She might be short of something.

Besides, Sharon had given him crabs. Thelma, with no fuss, had quietly got rid of the headlice the children brought home from school so she would certainly know what to do, whereas Sharon certainly didn't, otherwise why should she have them.

He was becoming sore from scratching. It took a lot of the lustre out of romantic love.

As well as that, he had an irresistible urge to sit for half an hour in his own fringed, moquette armchair, with the back door open and the smell of Thelma's sweetpeas drifting in from the garden.

❧

18

Frances wandered down to the playing field.

It was another hot afternoon. The sheep were repeating themselves monotonously. Somewhere a cock which had mistaken the time of day was crowing like somebody who has a good opinion of himself and fears he won't be applauded.

At the corner by the shop passers-by had stopped to observe the circus.

Endymion, clad in his father's pyjamas tied up with string, was climbing a ladder which had been placed between the ground and Blossom's fat back. An old sun hat of his mother's which was crammed down over his eyes obscured his vision and he was congratulating himself out loud each time he managed to find a rung with his foot.

'That's one up, that's another up, that's five up,' he chanted.

Martin and Hadrian and Andrew, all carrying ringmaster's whips constructed from garden bamboo poles and green twine taken from David's shed and bearing traces of yellow paint, wearing respectively, a black waistcoat from Joan's collection of things for the jumble sale, Alice's best black lurex evening blouse which she had not yet noticed as being absent from her wardrobe and Jeremiah's Sunday bowler were encouraging the pony to stand still long enough for Endymion to be installed, facing her tail, balancing on one leg until it was time for him to fall off into a paddling pool filled with water judiciously placed near by. He was being the clown.

Karen and two of her friends, liberally smeared about the face with lipstick, powder and green eyeshadow, were doing cartwheels up the bank. Karen was clad in one of the evening-gowns which Thelma had found in her attic. As she cartwheeled its voluminous chiffon skirt whirled round her thin brown legs like the blue petals of a sea flower opening and closing in the gentle movement of water.

'Eh, they're a quaint lot,' said deaf Aunt Ella. Deaf Aunt Ella remembered the days when children had their chores to do. 'Always up to something.'

'They're enjoying themselves,' Frances suggested.

'That's what they need,' agreed Aunt Ella, 'employment. Plenty of jobs about for them. Don't come and offer to whitestone my doorstep, I notice.'

Frances tried again.

'Playing together teaches them how to live together,' she said.

'All do it nowadays. No such thing as marriage any more. I hear that husband of Thelma Pickles is at it. Taken himself off with some lass doesn't know her arse from her elbow. All comes of not having enough to do. Had a fit, Agnes would have. It never rains but it pours.'

Frances wondered whether it would be possible to change the subject in such a way that Aunt Ella would notice the subject had been changed.

'It's a beautiful day,' she shouted into the old lady's ear.

'Too hot by far. Makes me sweat bobbers,' Aunt Ella replied.

There was a little ripple of clapping from the crowd as Endymion landed with a splash and came out dripping, his father's pyjamas clinging to him, a look of modest triumph on his face. Blossom had gone.

'Always ends like this. That Blossom. Takes so much and no more,' observed Mr Todd, retiring into his shop. 'Us old ones need a bit of consideration, or we get rattled. So much oining, and that's enough.'

Blossom was halfway up the next field. Two elderly horses who thought it was a game had cantered after her and thirteen or fourteen acrobats, clowns, fairies and ringmasters were scrambling over the wall of the playing field in pursuit.

'Spare the rod and spoil the child,' Aunt Ella said absently to nobody in particular.

Frances supposed that not having any children made one's view of them and their activities more tolerant than it might otherwise have been. She felt sure that if she and William had produced any they would have found life difficult, spreadeagled between the pillars of William's punctilious respectability and the tent poles of her enthusiasms.

But getting old changed everything anyway.

As Mr Todd said, so much oining and that's enough.

Though George, who had always been a tolerant man, had become more and more tolerant as the years passed, until in his last days he had lost contact with any of the standards against which things could be measured.

Leaving the group in the corner of the playing field, she walked slowly down the lane towards the reservoir.

George had been as wonderful when he was old as he had been when he was young or, at least, as young as he was when she could first remember him. Everything amused him. As he became old and senile, parts of his mind appeared to remain unimpaired. In the nursing home where he had spent the last year of his life he had made friends with Sam, an old soldier who was ninety. Sam had been batman to an officer in the First World War and George replaced his officer. Sam and George would sing the old war songs, George tapping out the rhythm with his stick and Sam conducting, a cigarette hanging from the corner of his mouth.

To the consternation of Hermione, who made it her duty to visit George every day, Sam and George would sing their own words to the old tunes. The young nurses liked these variations but Hermione would knit her lips into a disapproving shape and crochet like a Fury.

'It's a long way . . . to tickle Mary . . .' George would sing, out of tune.

'It's a long way . . . to the po . . .' Sam would add.

The old ladies and gentlemen sitting out on the patio of the nursing home would smile in the spring sunshine as if to embrace the song, the singers and the three lines of assorted vests and underpants doing a minuet in the faint breeze.

Or Sam and George would be raucous when wakening in the morning.

'It's a lovely morning, Sam. Done any flying lately?'

'We might take a spin this afternoon if the clouds keep high.'

Sam had been in the infantry. But he knew enough about officers and enough about flying to keep George happy. Not that George wasn't happy anyway, in his own little world.

'George,' one of the young nurses said, 'you've blocked the lavatory again. Why do you keep putting your socks down it?'

'I'm only posting them,' George pointed out reasonably.

'He just gets a bit mixed up,' Sam apologised. 'Letter boxes are for posting, George.'

'You don't put socks in letter boxes,' George replied patiently.

When you are old it is sometimes very difficult to make other people see sense.

Frances supposed that Albert was a substitute for George. Certainly he was very like him, calm, imperturbable, passionate with the gentle, philosophical generosity of real people. And for some unknown reason he loved her.

She walked past the sewage farm, its circular beds damped by sprays of water, its pipes and engines churning, emitting a faint hum in the warm air.

She could hear laughter from the field behind her. The circus was still endeavouring to recapture its star performer.

This was her village, her world. A crowd of rooks had gathered just beyond the sewage farm. They were discussing their housing problems in loud tones like magistrates arguing about the best punishment for an offender.

If only Hermione hadn't come to remind her of the past.

Frances sat down on a tree stump and looked towards the reservoir, flat and brilliant under the bright blue lid of the sky. Old age didn't matter here. People just became slightly odder and slightly frailer but nobody treated them any differently.

She wasn't sure that she wanted to get old. She might become like Hermione. Albert might become tired of her. She might lose her faculties, becoming deaf like Aunt Ella. She might start to criticise everybody and everything.

But it was so peaceful, so green, in spite of the dry weather. She stood up and stretched.

Then she wandered on, elation and depression struggling in her soul like two great, fat, sweaty wrestlers, listening to the sombre conversation of the rooks and the hysterical laughter of the children in the playing field where Andrew had mixed a large quantity of Howard's shaving soap, forgotten when he left home, into a rich lather and custard-pie throwing was now in progress.

19

Marcus was tired of the circus. They all made such a noise. Whatever they were doing they seemed to find it necessary to shout and laugh all the time.

When he laughed, he laughed inside.

Hadrian and Endymion called him 'Maggot'. 'Marcus the Maggot', they called him, because they said he was a bookworm. It had put him off books for a time until he realised that one seldom if ever came upon a worm in the pages of a book.

He was hot. There were no trees on the playing field. There was nowhere to retreat to. He thought he might spend the rest of the afternoon being a hobbit boy, perhaps Bilbo Baggins, and have an adventure.

He left the other children and began to walk down the lane. As he went an idea came into his mind, his developing mind stored with deep thoughts and interesting facts like Alice's.

Alice had told him that everything has a source, and that in order to appreciate things properly you have to find this. He knew, for instance, that the source of himself was partly in his father, David, whom he secretly thought of as Bungo, and partly in his mother, Alice, and that because these two loved each other and him he had grown in Alice's tummy and been born. The exact details were not yet clear in his mind, though it had something to do with rabbits.

Andrew had brought his rabbit in a carrier bag to visit their rabbit. It had been Endymion's idea. Andrew's rabbit, Semolina, was a doe. Their rabbit, Toad, so-called because he hopped like a toad, was a buck. They had put the two rabbits together in an enclosure on the grass which they constructed with deckchairs, an old table and pieces of David's shed which had dropped off at the back, and watched them mate. Later on Andrew's dad, who was not a friendly man like Bungo, had come to the door with three baby rabbits and suggested, rather unpleasantly Marcus thought, that Alice might like to find homes for these three as he understood that Toad had been the father and he was having to dispose of the other three. Alice hadn't known where to find homes for them as everybody seemed to have a rabbit already, so they had four rabbits now.

Still, he didn't think that David would have climbed on Alice's back like that.

He decided to find the source of the stream. For as long as he could remember, winter and summer, they had played in the stream. It was one of his best places. He should certainly know where it came from, where it began. The beginning of things held their secret. If he could find the source of the stream he would know something about it that nobody else knew. It would be a very special adventure, finding the source of the stream. And there were trees along the stream, so he could cool down.

He would know which way to go because the water ran away from the source. If he went upstream he would eventually come to it. When he was getting near to the source the stream would begin to get smaller. When he arrived there it would just be a little trickle of water, perhaps coming out of a magic rock or cave.

The more he thought about it the happier he felt. He was going to find the source of the stream. And the others didn't know anything about it.

As he trotted down the lane he noticed Frances ahead of him, inspecting something in her hand.

He liked Frances. She was like Alice. You didn't have to explain everything to her. He caught up with her.

Frances was examining some clover leaves.

'I thought I saw one with four leaves somewhere but when I bent down and picked them it disappeared,' she said to Marcus.

She pointed to a clump of clover.

Marcus crouched in the grass and peered through his spectacles at it. They all seemed to have only three leaves.

'Here it is. Here amongst these in my hand. I knew there was one,' Frances exclaimed.

Marcus felt a surge of excitement, like the water pulling back and then pushing forwards again when a wave is made. He was sweating. He rubbed his forehead with the bottom of his T-shirt. A four-leaf clover. That was what they called an omen. He could scarcely conceal his delight when Frances bent down and tucked the precious leaf into the band of his sun hat. He was so pleased that he almost gave away his secret.

'That will help,' he said gravely, 'that will help a lot. I'm going to the stream. I have to find out where it comes from. An adventure.'

Frances laughed.

But he knew that she wasn't laughing at him. She was laughing with him. She probably thought he was making a joke. Even the better grown-ups thought he was making jokes when he wasn't.

'Well, that should certainly be useful in an adventure,' she said.

He moved on, more quickly than before, knowing that he had almost said too much. Then he turned and waved.

'Thank you for the omen,' he called back.

Frances nodded, shading her eyes with her hand.

'Good luck,' she said.

Hadrian and Endymion referred to her as 'Old Frances Funny'. He didn't see anything funny about her. She was a lot more sensible than they were.

By the time he reached the stream he had become even hotter. So he took off his sandals and paddled. While he was paddling Aunt Ella's son Tom passed in his tractor. He waved to Marcus and Marcus waved back, standing with his hands on his hips in the water to admire those gigantic wheels which could travel across fields thick with mud into which an ordinary car, like Bungo's Renault, would have sunk right up to the top of its wheels, perhaps even up to the top of its roof.

He put his sandals back on and set off upstream.

It was cooler under the trees. The path went through woodland. Sometimes he had to climb and the stream vanished from sight for a few minutes. But it always came back again. Under the trees were dead, dry leaves from last year, and strange, whitish plants which grew where there wasn't much sun. There was a smell of soil and ferns, and the light came through the leaves overhead in long straight yellow bars, making him feel as if he were in a golden birdcage.

In an hour he had reached the furthest part he had ever been to, where the ford crossed the top road. From here onwards there was no proper path, just moorland with a few sheep tracks. There were no more trees, either, so he knew that he was going to get hot again. He also knew that this part of the adventure would be lonely. Until now he had been quite close to farms, to Tom's farm, to the farm from which they got the milk, where he had once seen a dead lamb, close even to the road which would have led him home if he had changed his mind about the adventure. Now he was going away from them all.

He didn't mind. You were more likely to meet a hobbit if you were quiet and alone.

The sun was making the top of his floppy hat red hot. He took it off to cool his head, noticing with relief that the four-leaf clover was still in place and not looking too bad, though it had grown smaller. He put his hat back on. Then he noticed that the back of his arms where they came out of his

T-shirt were burning. He stopped walking and plunged them into the water. Even the stream was warm. He took his sandals off and had another paddle.

Then he set off again. Now that he had reached proper moorland he had to climb real hills. Sometimes he lost sight of the stream and had to guess where it was. Sometimes he followed a sheep track which made the journey easier until it began to go in the wrong direction.

What puzzled him was the size of the stream. He would have thought that after so long it would be smaller. But it was still about the same size, and just as deep.

When he was going off to work in the morning Bungo used to say to Alice,

'A man's gotta do what a man's gotta do.' Then they both laughed.

He knew that he had to find the source, and partly it was a joke. But partly it wasn't. It seemed less funny when he realised that the sun was not so hot now, though his arms were still burning, that his calves and his knees ached and that his sandals had given him a blister.

He took off his spectacles and cleaned them on the leg of his shorts. They were all steamed up across the top half where they touched his eyebrows. When he had cleared them he looked around. Across the valley all he could see was tufts of grass, the odd rock, a few sheep which made him jump when they moved suddenly, and endless, endless sky, a sky becoming bluer and casting a strange light over the turf.

Marcus discovered that although he was still hot, the heat was no longer coming from outside himself.

He peered up the stream. Far ahead, in the distance, he could see the shape of a large cluster of black rocks. Alice had told him about the Ice Age, how the earth had been ploughed up and left in piles which became the hills and the valleys. But in his mind it was all becoming fused with his quest. Perhaps not the Ice Age but magic was responsible for that pile of rocks. Perhaps mysterious creatures with human intelligence had built that tower of stones. It could have been put there to tell travellers like himself that here was the source, the secret, the home of hobbits.

Setting off resolutely towards the pile of stones he felt elated in spite of his tiredness, pleased to think that his adventure was near its end. He would have such a lot to tell Hadrian and Dymmie. Though they never listened to him when he tried to tell them anything important.

A doubt crossed his mind. It would have been nice if they had been here with him now.

But no. This was his adventure. Endymion would have been saying that he was hungry. Hadrian would have been frightened because they were so far from the road.

It wouldn't take him as long to get back as it had taken him to get here. He would tell them all about it when it was over.

Marcus, of course, could tell the time. But he didn't yet possess a watch. So he didn't know that it was now three hours since he had waved to Tom from his first paddling stop at the end of the lane.

The last part of his journey was heavy-going. Between himself and the outcrop of rocks there was a great mass of bracken. In places this was higher than he was. He looked in vain for a sheep track and wished that he had brought Hadrian's penknife with him. If he had been careful not to cut himself and used it the way Bungo had taught him he could have cut some of this bracken down and got through it more easily. As it was he had to plough along, chest high. Tom's tractor would have gone through it like a sailing ship, one of the old ones with a high prow and a figurehead. Sometimes he lost sight of both the stream and the rocks for a few frightening seconds and only the thought of finding the source kept him going. He knew that there was something special there and he didn't have much further to go.

When he reached the rocks he was no longer hot. His spectacles were no longer misty. He sat down and looked at the water.

He saw, with dismay, that there was no magic cave, just a little space between the rocks from which the water crept like a tired small brother of itself, with no fuss and no splendour.

He was weary and he was disappointed. He took off his hat and looked at the wilted four-leaf clover. He had come a long way.

But it had been a good adventure. Marcus knew that there were no bad things in real life. The bad things only happened in books, and they always got better. So he wasn't afraid.

Soon it would stop being light. Perhaps the hobbits would come out then. He was tired. He would just have a little rest to give them a bit more time. Then he would go home.

He found a warm stone hollow lined with moss, dry and comfortable. He settled himself for his vigil and found that he was getting sleepy.

As if providing an overture to his drama the sky changed from its darkening blue to a deep crimson and set the grass, the rocks, the trickle of water and the little boy in a shimmering blaze of light.

20

Albert was thinking about Frances.

He was a meticulous man who, though retired, like to be able to account for his time. He had spent the morning talking on his amateur radio set to friends in Western Australia. Albert had friends all over the world. With these friends he passed many happy hours in deep conversation about the exploits of football teams, the Test, his mates and, most of all, the English weather. Albert was intensely interested in the weather. It seemed to confirm his moods in an uncanny way, exaggerating both his optimism and his pessimism. Then after lunch he had tied up his beans, which were doing well, and dozed in his deckchair under the poplar trees where there was some shade. Now he felt the need for some action.

He didn't really know what to make of Frances. Of course, he loved her. He loved her in a way that he hadn't loved a woman before. But in some ways you couldn't really regard Frances as a woman. Not that she was masculine. You could never mistake her for a man. Nevertheless she was more like a mate than a woman friend. He had said things to Frances that he would never have thought of saying to any other woman. She was totally contradictory and unpredictable, utterly feminine in that way, but also sensible in a curious, basic way, more sensible than most women were. And yet, having said that, she really wasn't a bit sensible. Impossible to understand what she was thinking about half the time. The effect she had on him, a staid, careful chap, was astonishing. Dreadful, really, when you thought about it. And she a respectable married woman. And neither of them exactly adolescent.

Albert put the deckchair away in his garden shed. He went into the house, locking the back door behind him. They had seen some beautiful rocks one day when they were walking up in the valley. This afternoon would be a good time to go and paint them. Frances liked painting rocks. Though when she had finished with them they would not look like rocks. They would be dancing about with a life of their own. Still, she would recreate the rockiness of rocks.

She was all over the place, Frances, yet she managed to draw things that resembled real things, even though they didn't look like them.

It was not his way of working. He liked to get it right. To do that you had to obey a hundred little laws of the eye and the hand, the space on the page, the tricks of light and shade, the subtle nuances of colour, the demands of perspective.

He filled the kettle, put some instant coffee into the big thermos flask and squeezed a packet of biscuits into the pocket at the side of his painting bag. While the kettle was boiling he dialled her number.

Telephoning Frances always caused him some anxiety. He was afraid that William might answer. It wasn't that he was afraid of William. On the contrary. He liked William, and he had a feeling that William liked him. He knew, rationally, that William did not mind him taking Frances out. In fact he was quite certain that William was glad about their friendship. After all, he was away much of the time. He had his own life and he seemed happy for Frances to have hers. It was difficult not to want Frances to be happy. When Frances was happy she made other people happy. William had lived with her long enough to know that. When Frances wasn't happy she was miserable. William was too good-natured himself to want anyone to be miserable. They were a weird couple, really. Very close, but not at all in each other's pockets.

No, it wasn't that he was afraid William would answer the telephone. After all, what would William be doing at home in the middle of the afternoon.

It was something that he couldn't explain. It had something to do with his sense that he and Frances belonged to each other and yet didn't belong to each other at all. He supposed he was just a conventional kind of fellow. But the thought of having Frances for a wife appalled him. She wasn't the sort of woman a man had for a wife. And yet he loved her and wanted to be sharing things with her.

He let the telephone ring twenty-five times just in case she was in the bathroom or out in the garden and then replaced the receiver with a sigh. If he didn't let himself think about her he could manage to go for several days without seeing her. But on those occasions when he decided to take her somewhere and she had already got it into her head to go somewhere else he felt a dark cloud descending upon him, as if they had been overtaken by bad weather on what had promised to be a beautiful day.

The kettle was boiling with venom. He made the coffee, locked the front door, placed his painting bag on the back seat of the car with the thermos flask and drove off towards the moorland road.

He'd just have to paint the rocks by himself. It was a pity. His picture with the picture that Frances would have painted would have made a better accounting of the afternoon than his would alone.

❦

21

'Was the circus still going on when you came back from your walk, Fran?' asked Joan, pouring more tea into the pretty flowered mugs on the round white metal table. They were sitting on her patio, now in the shade of the big sycamores which held the overcrowded rookery. Joan had scrubbed the paving stones vigorously but they still held a delicate yellow design of footprints, like petals, from Alice's painted feet.

'Full swing. Martin and Endymion were doing a balancing act on a plank between two buckets. Heaven knows where they get all their equipment from. It just seems to materialise.'

'Yes, and if I know anything, when tea time comes it will all be left where it drops and tonight half the village will be searching for its possessions and the old biddies complaining about the mess on the playing field.'

'It's worth the fuss, though, to have them enjoying themselves,' said Thelma gloomily, 'there'll be little enough for them when they grow up.'

Joan put her hand on Thelma's brown arm and patted it.

'Now don't look at it like that, dear. Think of me. I've been on my own since the week after Martin was born. I wouldn't have a man about the place again if you paid me.'

'You're used to it now, maybe. But what about at first? I keep thinking of things I want to say to him.'

Thelma had not yet revealed to Joan and Frances the thought she had entertained while she was walking down the hill. It seemed a bit off, trying to explain that though you had been abandoned, part of you felt very relieved by the abandonment.

'Write them down for when he comes back,' Frances suggested.

'Well, they're not the sort of things you can write down. I mean, we need some more toilet paper. He buys it in bulk at the supermarket. Things like that. Not very romantic.'

'If it hadn't been for the toilet paper he might not have left for his romance, from the sound of things,' Frances pointed out.

'Oh, that was only the deciding factor, seeing him doing the shopping. She had known him for years in the office. It just gave him another dimension, that was all. I suppose she had never realised before that he continued to exist after five o'clock, and there he was on a Saturday morning, all by himself with the toilet rolls,' Thelma explained.

'A challenge. They like a challenge, women of that sort,' said Joan, sitting rigid while a bee explored the regions around her left ear.

'Women of all sorts. We all make discoveries among the groceries. Very exciting, the supermarket. Like Aladdin's cave. Reminds you of things you haven't thought of for years. Gives you glimpses of the future. I never see a big yellow melon without thinking of my Aunt Clara.'

Joan looked at Thelma and Thelma looked at Joan.

'Not because she looked like a melon,' Frances continued hurriedly, 'but because she herself was in fact like a melon, blessed by the sun, firm, round and good.'

Frances had been having increasing trouble with her eyes as she grew older and, finding that she needed a new pair of spectacles and that the bill was going to come towards the end of the month when the allowance that William paid into her bank had run out, she had unwisely asked her mother for a loan.

'It's her latest fad,' Hermione had told Thelma, who was there at the time, 'thinking that she needs glasses. And of course Mother has to pay for them.'

'Well,' Thelma had thought, 'Frances is a bit vague about money. But she can't help not being able to see.'

'Was your Aunt Clara related to Hermione?' asked Joan,

who was somewhat in awe of Hermione – all that beautiful furniture, the old teacups in racks around the walls, the faded oriental rugs.

'Sister. Three of them. Elizabeth, the eldest, looked after Celia and Keith during the war. Clara had Nigel and me. Aunt Elizabeth was like Hermione. Clara was quite different. At least, Hermione is a lot of Elizabeth but I think also a bit of Clara. Can't find the bit of Clara but I'm sure it's there. Elizabeth had the temper and the autocratic ways. Good painter, though. Clara had the milk, or rather, the Scotch of human kindness. Couldn't paint though.' Frances puffed at a cigarette, vaguely aware that this little monologue had not explained her predicament.

Silence fell upon the three women.

It was quite true that Hermione was a cuss, Joan was thinking, but Frances did go on about her. And, after all, she only lived next door to Frances, not in the same house.

'We all have our problems,' said Thelma at length. Why did Frances not simply say to Hermione some of the things she said about her to her friends? The old lady probably had no idea how much she upset her daughter. She thought about Agnes and wondered that anyone could find their own mother a burden.

'Let's have another brew,' said Joan.

The summer air breathed gently in the shade among the lobelias blue as midnight, geraniums scarlet as dawn and the many-coloured pansies like mannequins in their velvet dresses.

The peace was shattered by an uproar in the street at the front of the houses and the children arrived.

'It's been the best circus we've ever had. We've made three pounds and thirty-five pence for the Blue Peter fund.' Karen was out of breath. She sat down on the wooden arm of her mother's garden chair. The make-up had been dispersed uniformly over her face leaving her a pale greenish colour like something accustomed to living several fathoms below the surface of the ocean.

Martin helped himself to three biscuits.

'What about the others?' Joan asked reprovingly.

Martin eyed the plate.

'I'll eat them later,' he replied.

'You know perfectly well what I mean. The other children.' Joan always fell right into it.

'Oh, sorry. Aunt Ella gave us most of it. Seventy-five pence.' He offered the plate to Hadrian, Endymion, Andrew and Karen.

'Her bark is worse than her bite. She was going on about "youth today" when I was down there earlier. But I think she's really rather fond of the kids. Wouldn't admit it, though,' said Thelma.

'Told me they never volunteered to whitestone her door-step.' Frances lit another cigarette. She smoked more when she was with other people. And it might discourage the bee that had been making advances to Joan's ear and was still hovering about looking for something to sting.

'They lived in hard times, I suppose,' said Thelma.

The biscuit plate was empty.

'Blossom kicked one of those old horses,' Endymion announced accusingly.

'It was an accident.' Karen was firm.

'It was not. She did it on purpose.'

'Didn't like it trying to get a piggyback ride,' Hadrian explained.

'Yes, it was doing what the cows do,' said Andrew.

'Would Blossom have had a foal?' Karen asked her mother.

'I would think she's past that. She's an old lady now. They would just be playing.'

'Aunt Ella said we should give her a treat for all her hard work,' said Hadrian.

'So we gave her a choc ice from Mr Todd's. That's why it was three pounds thirty-five. Otherwise it would have been three pounds fifty,' Endymion explained.

'Aunt Ella said horses don't eat choc ices but she did,' Karen added.

Nobody knew who's aunt Ella was but she was universally referred to in this manner.

'Perhaps not the best food for them,' Thelma murmured, licking the corner of her handkerchief and tentatively trying to remove some of the green from her daughter's face.

'Well, she was hot. And I'm hot.' Endymion lay down on his back on the patio. David's pyjamas had dried on him and now hung loose and dishevelled like the leaves on a small tree after a particularly bad thunderstorm.

The other children followed his example and the late afternoon sun descended on them all, a comfortable covering of hay smells, flower smells and the bewitching lights and colours which intermingled around them like a mediaeval wall-hanging.

Alice appeared in the doorway of her cottage.

'Hi, Mum,' said Hadrian.

'Hello, blossom,' Alice replied absently. She had been writing an article about the poets of the Romantic Revival. 'Oh, it's a party,' she exclaimed, coming back to earth and registering the gathering of her friends and children.

'Come and join us. I'll make another brew.' Joan pushed a chair into the shade of the trees and headed for her kitchen. 'Or would you rather have lemonade?'

'I'm not Blossom. I'm Hadrian,' said Hadrian, not thinking it would have been strange if his mother had mistaken him for the pony.

'Lemonade would be lovely.' Alice's long plait had become disorganised during her struggle with the Romantics.

'I suppose it will soon be tea time.' Joan disappeared into the shadow of the cottage.

Alice leaned back in the canvas chair. Frances thought how beautiful young people are, shining and pulsating and filled with a kind of languid vigour. Alice's hair fell all about her like a dark stretch of the stream.

'How are you getting on, dear?' Alice asked Thelma, suddenly remembering about Howard.

'Oh, we're all right.' Thelma blushed. Although she had come to talk about her problems, she did not particularly want to discuss them in front of her children. 'Well, I think it's time for us to make a move,' she added. She would come another day to discuss practical matters with Joan. Frances had given her some more money to tide her over. Mr Todd was going to put her groceries on the slate. She had never done this before but it was better than telling Fred. The gas bill would wait a bit longer.

There was a general stir. Endymion stood up.

'I'm going to tell Marcus Maggot that he missed seeing me dive into the bottomless pit from a wild horse,' he announced.

'I don't think you should call him that,' said Alice mildly. 'He doesn't much care for it.'

'Karen and Andrew, collect your dressing-up things.' Once Thelma decided to go she didn't linger.

Joan arrived with Alice's lemonade.

'Thanks for a lovely afternoon, Joan,' said Thelma. 'Come along, you two. Say goodbye to everyone.'

Endymion came out on to the patio.

'Marcus the Maggot isn't here,' he said.

'No, petal.' Alice was drinking her lemonade. 'He went to the circus.'

'He left the circus hours ago. We thought he was coming home.'

Hadrian stopped pushing Jeremiah's bowler hat down over Andrew's ears and considered his brother's absence.

Frances, carrying the mugs into Joan's kitchen, turned around.

'I met Marcus on his way down to the stream. We found a four-leaf clover.'

'Marcus likes things like that. The Mayor gave him a hen's foot once and he put it under his pillow because he thought it would give him good dreams.' Hadrian wondered where Marcus was. He had forgotten all about him. It was really his job to know where Marcus was.

'That's where he'll be,' said Alice comfortably. 'He'll be having a little adventure. You two go down to the stream and bring him home for tea, there's a lovely pair.'

'Do we have to? It's miles to the stream,' Endymion complained.

'Well, he does forget about time,' Alice apologised.

Hadrian decided to make it a race.

'Last one to the stream is a pig's tit,' he said.

'Hadrian, petal, I don't think you should use expressions

like that,' Alice said reproachfully. Though why not, private-
ly she couldn't imagine, except that when Martin used them
Joan objected and seemed to feel that Alice was in some way
to blame.

'All right. A cow's teat,' Hadrian compromised.

'It's too hot to run,' said Endymion and set off at a good
pace so that he had an unfair start on his brother which he
regarded as fair since Hadrian was bigger.

The children disappeared down the lane.

'How lovely it all is,' thought Frances, following slowly
with Thelma whose arms were piled with the obsolete
garments and on whose head reposed Jeremiah's bowler hat
once only seen on Sundays. Two old ladies passed them.

The air was filled with hay smells and hawthorn.

'It isn't everywhere that a woman could walk down the
main thoroughfare wearing an eighty-year-old bowler hat
and not cause a raised eyebrow,' Thelma whispered to
Frances, after returning the incurious 'good afternoon' of the
two old ladies.

'Just what I was thinking,' Frances replied.

She remembered that she would be alone tonight. She
would give Albert a ring and see whether he would like to go
for a walk later, much later, when the stars came out and the
moors were warm and mysterious as a mother's breast.

22

Hermione was looking out for Frances. She wished to tell her something. She wished to tell her what was preying on her mind. She wished to tell Frances that if she didn't take better care of William she might find herself in the monstrous regiment of women whose husbands had left them. That poor sister of Mr Pickles had tended her husband lovingly and he had gone off. What might William do, neglected and ill-treated as he was? The prospect for Frances was bleak indeed.

The problem of abandoned women had never seriously entered her consciousness before. She had not come across it in such an intimate way as she had this afternoon, with the Mayor's arm along the back of the bench and his earnest threats and lamentations sliding into her right ear.

She knew that George, no matter how hard-pressed he had been, would never have left her. Of course, he had always been well-looked after. Even during the days of the apron when there was a shortage of butlers, cooks, housemaids and gardeners she had always found just enough domestic help to enable her to keep George in the manner to which he was accustomed.

In any case, there was absolutely no reason why he should ever have preferred anyone else to her.

Now that the problem had entered her mind through the doorway of the Mayor's dilemma it sat there and grew like an unwelcome guest waxing fat on the contents of her mental larder.

It would be unfortunate, to say the least, if William were to leave Frances. If William were to leave Frances, Frances would have to leave the village. If Frances left the village she, Hermione, would be left alone, alone in this place where everyone dropped their empty crisp packets and coke tins as if the street were a giant dustbin – where there was no discipline and the drains smelled.

Of course, if Frances were not here the drains might improve.

She prepared a salad for herself and sat down at her glowing mahogany table to eat it. One must eat, no matter how upset one was. But her obsession was eating her, too. Since she returned from her walk she had been to her daughter's house three times to express this new fear to her and offer advice about how to avoid being left, but Frances, as usual, was out. Probably drinking tea with somebody.

How they all managed to drink so much tea was beyond her. Now that she was getting to know people she was often invited in for a cup of tea as she walked up the lane and she always had to explain that she only drank a cup of tea at four o'clock. Before that she abstained in anticipation. After that she remained dry for fear of having to get up during the night.

If there was one thing that Hermione hated it was having to get up during the night. She didn't sleep well. She lay awake for hours. While she was lying awake she would recite poetry to herself. She had learned a lot of poetry during her convent days. The nuns knew that poetry soothed the savage breast. While she lay awake it would not occur to her to get up and read, or, heaven forbid, make herself a drink. That was what education was for, to stock the mind so that when you were trapped by sleeplessness you didn't suffer from night starvation.

Frances said that she went to bed too early.

That was ridiculous, of course. As old Nanny used to say, 'early to bed, early to rise . . .' though she did sometimes wish those terrible birds wouldn't wake her at dawn. They sang in the silver birch tree and the oak tree in William's garden. Those two trees took up too much of the garden in any case. She had suggested many times that they should be cut down. But Frances said that they were symbols. The oak tree, which was sturdy and straight, represented William. The silver birch, which leaned precariously over the wall, represented her. They had planted them as seedlings after their honeymoon. Of course, Frances would have some obscure reason for not doing what would obviously be best for everyone.

Hermione kept an eye on the road as she ate. If Frances came from that poor Thelma's house she would see her pass the window. If she came from that nice Joan's house or the home of that impossible Alice, she wouldn't.

How could anybody bring children up the way Alice did. Behaving as if they should be consulted about how they spent their time. The noise they made down on the playing field. And the rubbish they left there. When she had passed it just now it had looked as if there had been a battle. Children should not be permitted to play unsupervised. Even if it was their playing field the rest of the village had to look at it.

As her salad reached its goal Hermione began to feel better. She had cooked herself a hard-boiled egg and covered it with mayonnaise and a daring dash of paprika. Food always brought out the best in Hermione. It brought to the surface the submarine qualities of Aunt Clara which Frances found so elusive.

Into her mind came an awareness of the Mayor.

He was such a nice man. Not educated, of course, but a gentleman.

It had been very agreeable, sitting on the bench talking to him. It had made her feel curiously young and happy. She was glad that she had been wearing that pink dress. He wouldn't know that she had possessed it for thirty years, since George took her to Spain. That had been a lovely summer too. The Mayor had asked her to go and have a cup of tea with him. She would certainly do so. The prospect of seeing the old barn filled her with excitement.

Of course, she would have to say no to the cup of tea, unless it was four o'clock. But she was sure he would understand.

Hermione's salad led her to remembering the strong warmth of his forearm along the back of the bench just touching her neck and shoulders. It led her to remembering his deep, musical voice.

You could tell a lot about people by their voices. People with tight voices usually led restricted lives. In the intellectual sense, that was. The Mayor's voice was resonant. The Mayor's voice was so resonant that she did not even object to his Lancashire accent. Hermione, still speaking with a Canadian accent after fifty years in Lancashire, felt qualified to castigate the natives, whom she accused of not speaking English properly.

The Mayor's confidence, too, had touched her. Not many people told her their troubles. She might, possibly, even have saved the life of that wretched brother-in-law of his by encouraging Mr Pickles to talk about him.

As she sat, her thoughts wandering pleasantly, the late afternoon stillness was shattered. Across the road, roaring up the hillside, through the field, their engines screaming, were three lads on motorcycles. Hermione's spleen poured back into her, leaving the bonhomie of the salad crushed and soured on its way into her intestines.

This was another thing she must mention to Frances.

There must be some law against riding motorcycles through the fields.

She would complain about it to Frances the moment she arrived home from wherever she had been wasting the afternoon.

23

Sitting on his low canvas painting-chair Albert held his picture out at arm's length to compare it with the landscape before him.

Of course, it was difficult to tell whether it was exactly right. The bright sunlight played havoc with colours. But on the whole he felt pleased with it. The rocks looked solid, the sky had turned out very well. You could never tell with skies. Sometimes the paint flowed and spread gloriously. Sometimes it wasn't wet enough and looked contrived. Sometimes it was too wet and made hollows in the paper as if a mischievous force had been sucking and blowing from the other side. His turf had turned out well, too, and the bracken. He hadn't overdone it this time. Just enough detail to suggest its disarray. Although there wasn't a breeze it was full of movement.

He had left his car drawn off the road and walked a quarter of a mile to where he remembered seeing the rocks and found them just as interesting as he had remembered them, their black horizontal and vertical masses piled by chance like misshapen dice hurled into the air and left where they had fallen.

He poured himself some coffee from the big thermos flask and, stretching out in his chair, ate a few of the biscuits. He half heard the plainsong of a peewit, the serenade of a couple of skylarks hovering like hidden minstrels somewhere overhead.

Pushing his hat to the back of his head he became Slam, ace reporter.

But it was no use. He couldn't have a case without his secretary, Slim.

So he closed his eyes and went to sleep.

24

It was when Andrew, Karen, Hadrian and Endymion returned from the stream having found no trace of Marcus that Slam's case began.

'Well, when did he leave the circus?' David was trying to conceal his anxiety and remain calm.

'I don't know what time it was.' Hadrian knew that David was anxious. If he had not been anxious he would have been angry. As the eldest it was Hadrian's responsibility to know where the others were. If David was anxious, Hadrian was very anxious. It would have been better if David had been angry. Then he would have known that everything was all right.

'It was before I dived,' Endymion volunteered. 'He was sitting by the wall looking down towards the stream not paying any attention to the circus when I dived. I know because I was high up and I could see across the field.' He had felt disappointed that Marcus had not seen his spectacular circus feat. It was hard to impress Marcus and he thought this might have done the trick.

'And what time was that?'

'I don't know. It was before the custard pies.'

'Didn't he tell you where he was going, that he was going off by himself?'

'No. One minute he was there and the next minute he wasn't. We were busy. We couldn't keep Blossom away from the grass. She kept having a little chew and we had to have her head up for Endymion's act.' Hadrian began to cry. 'He'll be all right, won't he, Dad? He'll be all right if he's lost?'

'He'll know where he is,' said Endymion. 'Marcus will know where he is. He won't be lost.'

'Yes, flower. But we want to know where he is, too, and bring him home.' Alice's usually rosy face was white as a magnolia blossom.

'Now let's be sensible about this. Who was the last person to speak to him?' asked David.

'Frances Funny saw him on his way down to the stream,' sobbed Hadrian, 'but we've been to the stream and looked everywhere and called him and he isn't there. He isn't anywhere there. And it's long past tea time.'

'And I'm hungry.' Endymion, though not yet anxious about Marcus, was beginning to be anxious about the absence of tea.

'I'll go down and see whether Frances can remember anything else that he said. Karen and Andrew, go home to your mother. Alice, give Hadrian and Dymmie some food. I'll be back soon. There's nothing else to do. He'll probably come wandering in any minute. If he does, Hadrian, you come down to Frances and William's house to tell me. No more tears. He's tough and it's a nice warm evening. I'm sure he's O.K.'

Frances opened the door.

'Oh, come in, David. Have a cup of tea,' she said happily. David wondered how many cups of tea Frances had drunk today.

She led him into the kitchen and cleared a space for him to sit down. She removed the remains of her meal from the table and began to fill the kettle.

'No thanks, Frances. I've just come to ask whether Marcus said anything when you saw him going to the stream. I mean, anything which would tell us where he might be. He hasn't come home.'

'Oh David, hasn't anyone seen him since then? It was half-past two when I went out. I watched the circus. I walked down the lane. I stopped and talked to Aunt Ella. It must

have been about three when we found a four-leaf clover.'
That's four hours ago. A little chap like Marcus missing for
four hours. He could be anywhere. 'He could be anywhere.'

As soon as she had expressed this thought she felt better.

'He'll be at one of the farms, David. He'll be at Tom's, or
he'll have gone to watch the milking. Somebody will be
looking after him. You know Marcus.'

'I've phoned all the farms,' David said, 'and Tom saw him
down at the stream but he only waved. Said he was paddling.'

Frances sat down. A shadowy memory was stirring in the
shrubbery of impressions she had collected during the afternoon.

'We laughed. He said something about an adventure.' If
only her memory had been better. It was so awful to know
that you knew something and not be able to remember it. If
only she didn't clutter herself up with so many unimportant
things. She remembered the way Aunt Ella's neck had two
folds of skin which went from her chin to the front of her
blouse in straight lines like sagging telephone wires.

'Wait a minute, David. He said he was going to see where
the stream came from. That was what made me laugh. I
thought of him plodding halfway to Yorkshire . . .' she
stopped.

'Little sod,' said David. 'He always has to find out where
things come from. He'll have gone upstream. As long as he
has stuck to the stream he'll be all right. He's probably got
tired and sat down to wait for us. Thanks, Frances. We'll go
and find him.' As long as he has stuck to the stream. As long
as he has stuck to the stream.

Frances saw Marcus sitting by the stream. But where? How
far had he gone? If he had kept going, by this time he could be
out on the moorland. Albert had often taken her up there in
his car. Once you left the road you could be lost within a few
minutes. There were no landmarks, no paths except sheep-
tracks wandering aimlessly backwards and forwards on
themselves. There weren't even any walls which led anywhere. Just turf and sky.

'I put the four-leaf clover in his hat band,' she said.

David smiled.

'Marcus likes that sort of thing. If he is lost it will comfort him. More likely he's just waiting for us to come and get him. He has a touching faith in magic, my son Marcus. Thinks destiny leads him.'

'Shall I come with you? William isn't coming home tonight. The more people you have, the better.'

'No, you stay here. Go up and keep Alice company. That would be a help. Hadrian is upset.'

There came a sharp knock on the door, commanding as the single flash of lightning which presages the first rumble of thunder.

Hermione walked in.

'Ah, there you are. I've been looking out for you.' Drinking tea in the kitchen with a man, as usual. Doesn't anybody in this village ever do anything except drink tea in the kitchen? Ignoring David she continued, 'Frances, I would like a word with you, when you have finished drinking your tea.'

'We're not drinking tea.' Frances thought this point was worth making.

'I'll go then. And thanks, Frances. Tell Alice I'm walking up the stream. Tom said he'd come if we had to go looking for him, and Mr Todd's son Alan is at home. He knows the place inside out.'

'Will you, er . . . will you need torches?' Frances hesitated, thinking of lights flickering in the darkness like glow-worms, sombre figures swishing at the bracken with sticks, police, tracker dogs.

'We'll start off as we are. He's probably only at the ford.'

'What's all this about?' Hermione demanded when David had gone.

'Alice and David's little boy is missing.'

'Endymion? He's no great loss, if they don't find him.'

'It isn't Endymion. It's Marcus.'

'People with too many children can't control them. I'm not surprised. That Alice. Too much brain and no common-sense.'

'Mother.' Frances felt the hatred from the peach. 'Mother.

You are the one who is supposed to be so keen on education. Alice has a B.A., an M.A. and a Ph.D. I don't know what more you want from her.'

'Then she should have stuck to her books, not gone in for dozens of children she couldn't look after properly.'

'You had more than she has.'

'I had people, qualified people, to look after them.'

'Alice only has three and she looks after them, herself, very well.'

'I don't call losing them on the moors when they should be in bed looking after them well. In any case, that's no concern of mine. I just came to say that I have been thinking about you and William.'

'Well, you go on thinking about me and William. I'm going up to sit with Alice.' Frances slammed the front door.

Hermione sat down on a chair which already contained all last week's newspapers and a collection of ferns, waiting to be dried for decoration in the winter.

Really, Frances was so rude. What had she said to deserve a retort like that?

25

As Thelma entered her house she had a feeling that something was different. What was different was the presence of Howard. She wasn't sure how to cope with this difference.

'Hello, Thelma,' said Howard ingratiatingly.

He wondered why she was wearing a bowler hat. He wondered why she had her arms full of old clothes.

Could she have been driven to selling things?

A terrible wave of guilt engulfed him. It knocked him off his feet. Metaphorically, that is. He was sitting in his fringed moquette armchair.

Thelma decided not to make a fuss.

'I suppose you'll want some tea,' she said. 'We're late. The children have gone down to the stream to fetch Marcus home.'

'Well, I've eaten,' said Howard doubtfully, finding himself, in spite of being in love with a younger, more attractive, more vivacious woman, wondering wistfully what Thelma was going to produce for tea. 'I've come to give you some money. And to have a talk. We must get things sorted out. Make proper arrangements, if you see what I mean.'

She hadn't fallen into his arms. Why didn't she make a scene, beg him to come home, tell him that she couldn't live without him?

Thelma went to the kitchen. In spite of herself she found that she was glad to see him. She was going to cry, and she didn't want Howard to see her cry.

It was the relief. She would be able to pay the gas bill. She could give some money back to Frances. She wouldn't have to put things on the slate at Mr Todd's.

Howard followed her into the kitchen. He noticed that she had made a fruit loaf. In spite of the chips without curry he suddenly felt very hungry.

Thelma wiped her eyes.

'Do you want a piece of cake?' she asked.

'I wouldn't mind.' Howard tried to sound casual.

Thelma busied herself.

Howard sat down at the kitchen table and devoured his cake, eating as slowly as it was possible for him to eat in the circumstances.

The back door crashed open and Karen and Andrew had arrived.

'Marcus is lost. He's not down at the stream. Hadrian is crying,' Andrew announced. Mind you, Hadrian cried a lot. He cried when they caught a fish. They were going to put it back but they couldn't get the hook out of its jaw. So Andrew killed it with a stone. It had taken a long time to stop flapping. Hadrian said he was cruel. But you can't put a fish back with a hook in its mouth. Marcus said sometimes you have to be cruel to be kind.

'Well, it's his own silly fault,' said Karen, 'he's supposed to know where Marcus is.'

Thelma set three places at the kitchen table around Howard.

She didn't know where to turn her thoughts. There was a sunny patch in her mind where the knowledge that she was going to have some money was situated, and there was the less sunny patch in which Howard was sitting eating a piece of his favourite cake, and there was the absolutely black patch where her fears for the safety of little Marcus lurked with ominous, staring eyes.

'Wash some of that mud off, love,' she said to Andrew. 'Come here and let me wipe your face, Karen. You're all green still.'

They sat down at the table.

Howard looked at the food and ate the last crumbs of his cake.

'Do you want some of this?' asked Thelma, following his eyes.

If he said yes when he had already told her that he had eaten she would think he wasn't being fed properly.

'No, it's all right,' he replied in a strangled voice.

Thelma and the children ate in silence.

'Well,' said Howard brightly, 'and how are we all?'

'We've had a circus,' Andrew replied with his mouth full, 'that's when Marcus got lost.'

'Blossom ran away. Marcus had gone before Endymion did his best trick. We were the acrobats,' Karen added.

Howard felt slightly uncomfortable. He didn't know what he had expected. Perhaps he had hoped for a big emotional scene. Perhaps he would have liked it if the children had wept and begged him to come back home to live. Perhaps he had thought they would appear more grief-stricken than they were.

None of them showed any sign of having noticed that he had not been there. All they could talk about was Marcus.

He wondered vaguely how many rabbits there were in that family now.

'Eat your lettuce, Andrew,' said Thelma sharply.

'I don't like lettuce.'

'Eat it anyway. It won't take a minute to go down. You haven't had any vegetables today,' she added more gently. Alice wouldn't have shouted at him. Alice would have explained about vitamins and roughage.

Poor Alice. She must be frantic.

Howard scratched himself discreetly under the table. This was obviously not going to be the visit in which to consult Thelma about the disposal of crabs. He stood up and wandered back to his moquette armchair in the sitting room.

It had all gone wrong. He had come home for solace and comfort. Instead of a peaceful lagoon he had found a sea of troubles. He sighed and took his wallet out of his back pocket. He selected two twenty-pound notes and three tens. He shuffled them together and placed them conspicuously on the glass-topped coffee table.

He could hear his wife washing up noisily.

He leaned back in his armchair, looking around with pleasure at the furnishings of his home, the hunting prints bought when they were on holiday in Scarborough, the plaster and gilt mirror given to them by Agnes as a wedding present, the chrome standard lamp, the artificial flower arrangement from the Harvest Fair. It had been created by one of the ladies from the chapel and Howard had gone back and bought it for Thelma as a surprise after she had admired it.

'Dad,' Andrew asked, coming from the kitchen, 'if it was me lost, would you come and look for me?'

Howard changed his mental gears with a terrible grinding.

'Well, of course I would, son,' he replied.

'How could you when you are never here?'

'I'd come home, of course.'

'How could you know that I was lost?'

'Your mother would tell me.'

'How could she tell you when she never knows where you are?'

'She would telephone me at the office.'

'You might not be at the office when I got lost.'

'I'm at the office every day.'

'But it's night now. I might have starved to death.'

Howard scratched his head. Then he scratched his crotch.

'There are lots of people who would be looking for you. I'd come as soon as I heard about you being lost. Anyway, you aren't lost so the question doesn't arise.'

'Marcus wasn't lost until this afternoon.' Andrew took a tin of wax crayons out of the drawer in the teak wall unit and began to rub them furiously on a wad of paper. He produced a thick layer of multi-coloured wax which he then proceeded to scrape at with the point of an empty biro.

'Don't do that in here, son,' Howard said automatically, 'you'll get wax on the carpet.'

Andrew took his pattern into the kitchen.

'Well I'm glad it's not me,' he said, closing the door.

Howard thought about Sharon's body, her slim, suntanned body, her long blonde hair, her elegant fingernails painted dark red, her faintly bestial smell, in spite of perfumes. He thought about her carefree attitude towards other people, her inability to appreciate their problems, her taut, demanding urgency when they made love.

That was the way to be. We all have to live our own lives. No point worrying about anyone else.

He thought about himself when he was a lad. His father had always been too drunk to understand what he was saying, his mother too busy, too tired or too anxious to listen. That was the way it was. You had to do the best you could for yourself. No good trying to look after everyone. Even a wife and children complicated things intolerably.

He could hear Thelma putting the plates away. She would come into the sitting room in a minute.

Howard decided that he didn't want to see her. That little cry had made her face look puffy. Karen had gone upstairs. He knew that he had nothing to say to his daughter. He couldn't be bothered with her chatter. In any case, they were all more concerned with the missing child than they were with him.

He took two more ten-pound notes out of his wallet, anchored them on top of the others with the onyx table lighter and left, closing the front door quietly behind him. He would come back another day to talk to Thelma when she was less preoccupied.

Changing his mind halfway down the front path he returned without making a sound. He picked up the onyx table lighter and put it into his jacket pocket, then let himself out again.

It was his, anyway. She had given it to him for Christmas the year they were married.

26

'Haven't seen Alice and David's boy, I suppose?' Mr Todd asked casually, turning the tap on the barrel full to facilitate the flow of diesel into the Mayor's bottle.

'That young Endlemon?' asked the Mayor. 'He missing?'

'Not Endymion. The little one. Marcus. Hasn't been seen since three o'clock.'

'Can't say I have. Had other things on my mind. Hasn't been to the farm.'

'My Alan and Tom Hartley gone up the stream with his dad looking for him.'

The Mayor consulted his watch. It was eight o'clock.

'Late for a little lad to be about on his own. If it had been that Endlemon I wouldn't have been surprised. A bugger, yon. Little one's quiet I always thought.'

'It's the quiet ones you've got to watch,' said Mr Todd morosely. 'The others you can see what they're up to.'

The Mayor accepted his tumbler of diesel for testing. He poured it down his throat.

'Aye. That'll do nicely, thank you kindly,' he said. 'Mind you, if it had been that Endlemon I'd have said it wasn't a big loss,' he added reflectively, echoing Hermione's sentiment. 'I'll look out for him though.'

By a strange coincidence he was also thinking about Hermione as he trundled back up the hill to the farm on his ancient tractor, his diesel firmly wedged against the engine.

He felt warm but not hot, kind but not silly; comfortable in his mind. Extra comfortable in his mind. He would go and see Thelma tomorrow to find out how she was getting on.

Also, he would ask her to bake him a date loaf. He must be prepared. He was expecting a visitor one day soon.

A lady visitor.

27

David drove to the ford in his Renault. Tom and Alan had started walking upstream from the spot where Marcus had been paddling when Tom waved to him. They had agreed to meet back at the ford.

It was unthinkable that the child had gone further than this. David drew off the road into the gateway of a field and gazed up towards the rugged, barren moorland. But it wouldn't do any harm to go on. If he was somewhere between the village and the ford Tom and Alan would find him. He could be playing in the woods, building himself a Tigger house or looking for some mysterious treasure. He could have fallen asleep in the heat. Whatever he was doing he would be totally absorbed in the enterprise. Even if he had fallen asleep there would be some significance in any dream that he encountered. Marcus was one long stream of consciousness.

The stream. It was a long stream, too. He had told Frances that he was going to find out where it came from.

David was engaged in a struggle with his own stream of consciousness. He was trying to dismiss from it ideas of child molesters, falls, broken limbs, fractured skulls, misadventure of all kinds. These ideas crowded into his thoughts like football hooligans – loud, vicious, bent on destruction.

Working for a newspaper, he was only too familiar with the subjects their presence raised. They surged backwards and forwards in his mind, notions of cruelty, disaster, death.

Little Marcus. Little Marcus who was so like Alice, so placid, so trusting, so full of innocent wisdom.

He began to feel the inescapable fingers of panic.

He made his way upstream, calling his son's name in a hoarse voice. If he had come as far as this it should be easy to find him. There were no trees to hide him, to distract him from the presence of the stream. As long as he had stuck to the stream. He must surely have stuck to the stream.

The sky had become a deeper blue and David knew that before long it would redden and then begin to grow dark. Perhaps they should have brought torches. No, he would walk for a couple of miles and then come back to the ford. Tom and Alan would be there waiting for him with Marcus. If they were there without Marcus and he had not found him either they would drive back to the village and telephone for police help.

Police help. He began to sweat. Into the mob in his mind marched uniformed men with sticks and dogs, beating the turf, searching for clues, rows of men systematically eliminating places where a small boy, or the body of a small boy, might be found. He saw long lines of lights hovering up and down in the hollows of the moorland, heard the whining and yapping of Alsatians. He walked as quickly as he could, calling again and again, his throat dry, his thoughts running out of control.

'Tragic death of five-year-old.' The headlines appeared in a hundred different forms. 'Small boy's adventure ends in tragedy. Mother fails to notice son is missing.' A brief moment of rage possessed him. Why had Alice allowed him to be away alone for so long? She should have known where he was. She knew Marcus well enough to have guessed that he wouldn't stay at the circus for long. She was a hopeless mother. But as soon as the moment came it had gone again, like the passing of a comet, bright and angry for a few seconds, then dead.

Alice was not a hopeless mother. She was one of the best mothers he knew. She was bringing his sons up to think for themselves, to be curious, to follow through their own ideas. This did not produce the same immediate effect as the rigid disciplines of people like Joan. But Alice and he both knew that in the long run Hadrian, Endymion and Marcus would benefit from her method. When they did grow up – he would not allow the thought 'if they grew up' to pass the gates of his mind – they would be socially responsible men. He thought about the gossip and the criticism which their attitude provoked and felt a sense of despair as he climbed the hills, sometimes losing sight of the stream, thinking that Marcus could not possibly have come as far as this, thinking of the child's small legs and his huge, determined will.

It occurred to him that we tailor our lives to fit the smallest minds in the community. Nobody else would view this episode, however it ended, as a part of the essential Marcus. It would just be regarded as a case of deplorable negligence.

He sat down on a rock by the stream to catch his breath, still calling Marcus in a strange voice unlike his own. The only sound he heard in response was the faint sigh of a small breeze which barely stirred the reeds along the bank.

The sky began to turn red and the water grew crimson and black. Crimson and black. The colours of violence and death.

He must have come about two miles by now. He would go back. Marcus would be waiting for him at the ford with Tom and Alan.

If he wasn't, the sooner they telephoned the police the better.

He stood up, wiping the sweat from his forehead with the sleeve of his shirt, and started back along the stream towards the rapidly falling red coal which was the sun.

28

When Albert woke up the sun had set. He reached for his hat which had fallen off, stood up, stretched his legs and looked around.

It was not yet dark. The sky was still full of colour, but the colour was nebulous and subdued, twitching and nervous as a stray cat wandering over the landscape. He could still see the rocks but they were just a black shape now. All the ledges and angles that he had drawn so carefully earlier in the day were obscured by the beginnings of the summer night. A few clear stars gleamed self-consciously in the tabby sky, aware that they had arrived at the party too early.

He decided that he would walk down to the rocks and have a slash.

As he stood between the rough, warm greenish stones performing this function he became aware of a small, pale face watching him intently.

Albert knew all about young creatures, both dumb wild ones and gifted human ones. Softly, softly. You mustn't ever hurry or show that you were surprised. Without turning to look properly at his observer he said casually, 'I'm just having a jimmy-riddle.'

'I see,' said Marcus, adjusting his glasses. It was a strange place to be doing what he was doing. Though Endymion did it all the time, wherever he went. He wondered who Jimmy Riddle was.

'Jimmy-riddle. Piddle,' explained Albert, sensing the question and concluding his task. He turned and examined his companion in this isolated spot.

As Albert did not live in the village he did not recognise Marcus. But he knew that at eight o'clock at night it was a strange setting for such a small boy, apparently alone. In the fading light he could see that the child's arms and legs were scratched all over. He was wearing a sun hat with what looked like a caterpillar crawling out of its band.

'Where have you come from?' asked Albert.

This was the sort of question Marcus liked. He liked it when people asked interesting questions, not obvious ones.

'Well, I came partly from my mother and partly from my father,' he explained. 'Because they loved each other and me I grew in my mother's tummy and was born.' He stopped. He didn't want to admit to this person that the details were not yet clear in his mind, and the story of the rabbits was too long to tell just at the moment.

It was Albert's turn.

'I see,' he said. He pushed his hat to the back of his head. 'And where have you come from since then? This afternoon, for instance.'

'Up the stream.' Marcus thought this was an obvious question but he was too polite to say so.

'Where were you when you started up the stream?'

'Down the lane past the playing field.'

'Have you come all the way from Medwell? By yourself?'

'Yes and I've found the source of the stream.' Marcus modestly indicated the trickle of water muttering and chuntering from the gap in the rocks.

Albert could see that this was important. Ten yards upstream, before it plunged underground to emerge from the rocks in a trickle, the water was still running in a fairly strong torrent. He decided not to mention it. Marcus, having reached the rocks, had obviously not investigated any further.

'So you came all this way and found the source of the stream.' He knew that somebody must be looking for this adventurer and thought that they should spend as little time as possible on formalities. 'Well, I think I'd better take you home now.'

Marcus peered at Albert through the dusk. Albert's face was dark from the sun but he could see that it was all wrinkled and smiling.

'Are you a hobbit?' he asked.

'No, I'm not one of those. I'm an Albert,' Albert replied. 'What are you?'

'I'm a Marcus,' Marcus said, pleased by Albert's little joke. 'But I'm not allowed to go anywhere with people I don't know.' It would be nice to get home. He was rather tired. A hobbit would have served two purposes, both to hallow the source of the stream and to take him home.

'Perhaps I could be a part-time one of those. Hobbits,' suggested Albert, stretching out his hand to Marcus who was still sitting in his cosy hollow with his arms folded around his knees.

Marcus took Albert's hand and pulled himself to his feet. His legs ached.

'What do they call your dad and mum?' asked Albert, seeing a way out of the dilemma.

'David is my father and Alice is my mother,' Marcus reported earnestly.

'Then that's all right,' said Albert. 'I've heard my friend Frances talk about David and Alice, so you and I know each other.'

Marcus felt a surge of relief.

'Oh, I know Frances,' he exclaimed. 'She gave me this when I was setting off.' He removed his hat and took the curled up caterpillar out of its band. 'It's a four-leaf clover.'

'Then that's been lucky for both of us. So I'll take you back to David and Alice now and you'll have a ride in my car and I'll have the pleasure of your company for the journey.'

They stumbled back across the moorland to Albert's chair and painting bag.

'Oh, that's why you were here. I was wondering,' said Marcus.

'Been painting a picture of those rocks of yours,' Albert explained. 'Fell asleep.'

'I fell asleep too. Waiting for the hobbits.'

'Would you like a biscuit? And a little drink of coffee?'

They had a brief picnic in the gloaming, Albert carefully pouring the last of the coffee into the lid of the thermos flask and watching Marcus swallow it and several biscuits.

'This is a celebration,' Marcus announced. He had only just noticed, as he drank Albert's coffee and ate Albert's biscuits, that he was hungry.

'Finish the biscuits as we go,' Albert suggested. 'We've got a bit of a walk to the car. Think you can make it?'

Marcus had a sinking feeling, as if after a long swim he had dragged himself on to a raft and found that it was beginning to go down.

'Oh yes,' he said gamely.

Albert hitched his painting bag on to his shoulder, tucked his chair and the thermos flask under his arm and took Marcus by the hand. If the going got too bad he could carry him under the other arm for a few yards at once.

By the time they reached the road Marcus was finding it difficult to walk. He stumbled several times and would have fallen if Albert had not been holding him up.

He lay down on the back seat of Albert's car and closed his eyes.

Albert switched on his headlights and drove as fast as he dared along the narrow road. Sweat poured down the sides of his face.

If he hadn't come out this afternoon the child could have been alone all night. He shivered. He knew where Alice and David lived, in one of those cottages halfway up the hill. He would deliver the child and then go and call on Frances. She had said that William was going to be away for a few days.

He might be able to persuade her to put the kettle on.

29

❦

David returned home grimly conscious that he must now inform the police. At the ford Alan and Tom had been waiting for him without Marcus.

He put his arms around Alice who was crying helplessly. Hadrian and Endymion had been sent upstairs to bed and come down again. Frances was hovering about trying not to let her own anxiety add to the sum of grief which already filled the kitchen.

'Marcus hasn't had any tea,' said Endymion helpfully.

'He'll have some when he comes home.' David was firm. 'Now you two lads go back upstairs. It's getting late.'

'Can I come with you to look for Marcus?' Hadrian was now beside himself with the guilty feeling that all this, Alice crying, David not being angry, was his fault.

'No. Now stop worrying, Hadrian. It's nobody's fault. People like Marcus get themselves into situations like this. You couldn't be expected to know what was going on in his head. Nobody could. Now go upstairs to bed. When you get up in the morning he'll be sitting here eating his breakfast as usual.'

David wished that he could feel as confident as he sounded.

'I'll just make some tea,' said Frances awkwardly. She felt that she was in the way. But if David went out again with the police Alice would be alone again. And if the boys were going to reappear downstairs every quarter of an hour she knew that they would be less upset by Alice's state if she were there.

'Good idea, Fran,' said David. I could do with some tea. I'll just go and make my telephone call and then we'll all have a brew while we wait for the police.'

He went into the little room next to the kitchen.

Hadrian and Endymion were sitting side by side on the leather sofa. Between them a pale yellow angel spread its wings.

'If Marcus is dead will he be in heaven yet?' Endymion asked.

'Endymion. Will you go upstairs. For the last time. I'm telling you. Go to bed.' David pointed commandingly at the stairs.

Hadrian felt better. Dad was angry.

It was during the moment when Frances was silently pouring three mugs of tea and Hadrian and Endymion were taking a last curious look at Alice weeping from the doorway into the kitchen and David's trembling finger was dialling the last of three nines that the back door opened.

'Ah, you're here,' said Albert to Frances, 'I've been telephoning you all afternoon.'

'He isn't a hobbit,' Marcus added, 'but he brought me home because we're friends.'

'David,' Alice screamed, 'David, he's here.' She flung her arms around Marcus and hugged him to her.

Marcus, visibly moved by the atmosphere in the kitchen, blinking in the bright light, cleared his throat and struggled with the need to shed a few tears.

David rushed into the kitchen.

'Bungo,' said Marcus, forgetting, holding out his arms.

There was a scene of great rejoicing.

'Have you had a lovely adventure?' Alice asked, wiping her own eyes, wiping Marcus's eyes, wiping his nose, wiping his dirty face, wiping her own eyes again.

'It isn't as special as I thought it would be,' Marcus said regretfully, 'but I found it.'

'Marcus,' said David, in a choked voice, 'Marcus, will you promise me that the next time you have a big idea you will discuss it with Alice first?'

Endymion wondered whether this was the moment to describe his dive to his younger brother. He decided that it wasn't. He'd tell him in the morning when the fuss had died down.

Albert and Frances looked at each other. It was a beautiful night. The stars were now fully at their ease. The moon was playing the expansive host. The summer air had enjoyed a few drinks.

'Aye,' Albert said to David, 'it was a lucky thing all round. Me painting the rocks today and young Marcus ending his safari there.' He had an idea. Excusing himself he went out to his car. He returned with the painting of the rocks. It was a tender, delicate picture, the grass and the bracken just right, the rocks vibrant with hope, the sky as wide and blue as the aspirations of childhood. He handed it to Marcus.

'Now, if anybody doubts where you've been, you show them that,' he said.

'Is it mine?' asked Marcus.

'It's yours,' Albert replied expansively. 'Pin it on the wall of your bedroom. And the next time you get the notion to go there, be sure you take somebody with you.'

Alice and David were thanking Albert, thanking Frances, trying to get the children to go upstairs, keeping them down a bit longer to hear some more of the story, kissing each other, kissing Marcus, kissing Hadrian and Endymion, wringing Albert by the hand, exclaiming about the good fortune that had brought Albert out to paint on the day that had taken Marcus out to explore, exclaiming that it was getting late, exclaiming that it was all so lovely.

David telephoned Tom and Alan and told them that Marcus had returned.

Endymion, looking at the clock, said, 'Is Marcus going to have his tea now? I'd like some more tea.'

Frances and Albert thought they would leave this happy scene. There was nothing else for them to do here.

And the moorland, slightly tipsy with excitement, was beckoning them.

They said good-night and drove back along the narrow road to the scene of the adventure. It was now clad in a negligée of purest silver, the grass silver, the stream silver, the humpy, provocative rocks silver, the sky silver with a flush of stars and the rollicking moon.

Albert pushed his hat to the back of his head.

'That's where I found him, Slim,' he said, pointing to the little hollow in which Marcus had lodged.

Frances took a deep drink of the moonlight.

'Pity he couldn't have seen it like this,' she murmured.

'He will, one day. He'll be up here, like me, with a gorgeous woman, wondering what to do next.'

Somehow it didn't seem necessary to make a big decision about this.

They accommodated themselves comfortably below the enchanted rocks on the turf which was still warm from the day's heat. The breeze had gone to sleep and the world breathed gently in and out under the black, sparkling sky while Albert and Frances made love with that unhurried thoroughness which is granted only to those who are on their way back down the hillsides of experience.

30

If anyone else mentioned Marcus Entwistle Hermione would scream.

Every time she had been to her front door all morning somebody had stopped and said wasn't it a fortunate event, that friend of Frances's finding him up on the moors. As far as she was concerned the whole episode was disgraceful and should be swept under the carpet without more ado.

In any case, she had more important things on her mind. She had been trying to catch Frances to tell her about a letter she had received in the post. Her old schoolfriend Freda had written to say that she was coming to England and intended to stay with Hermione. She was coming next week and wondered whether Hermione would make arrangements for them both to have a holiday in Scotland.

So inconsiderate. As if she could possibly make arrangements for them to have a holiday in Scotland. Wasn't that just like Freda? Wave your wand, Hermione, and arrange a holiday in Scotland. Then there was the question of meeting Freda in Manchester. Freda's plane was due to land at half-past six in the morning. Freda had said that she would come to Medwell by taxi but of course they couldn't let her do that. Nigel would have to go. She certainly wasn't travelling to Manchester at that hour in the morning.

In short, Hermione was in a thoroughly bad mood.

She decided that if Frances wasn't awake yet it was high time somebody woke her. She knocked imperiously, then tried the door. It was locked. She knocked imperially then stood with her arms folded across her chest.

Frances, clad in a dressing gown from which the left sleeve had become partially detached, unlocked it.

'I've been awake since half-past five,' Hermione said by way of greeting.

'I've been asleep since then,' Frances replied, thinking about Albert's legs in the light of the rising sun under the magic rocks. Albert always said that women were jealous of his legs. Frances didn't know why. She wouldn't want to have Albert's legs. They were very nice legs, but definitely a man's. Very nice to be crushed up against and wound around by, but not the sort a woman would want to be pulling tights over when she got dressed. Albert's legs had the same texture as the turf, the same earthy spring and verve, the same way of enclosing you completely and providing for all your needs, as the womb encloses and provides for the baby.

'Well, it's time you were awake now.' Hermione was not going to stand for any nonsense. Really, Frances was a middle-aged delinquent. Where had she been until half-past five in the morning? Not at home. She knew that, because she had been back several times to see whether Frances had returned from that Alice's. And as she was opening her curtains at half-past five she had happened to notice that Mr What's-his-name's car cruising to a halt outside William's house. That was the other thing she had wanted to talk to Frances about. William. But the talk about William and the way Frances treated him would have to wait. This was more urgent.

'Do you want to come in?' Frances asked, yawning. She knew there was no point in offering Hermione a cup of tea.

'I've had a letter from Freda. She's coming for a holiday,' Hermione announced in furious tones.

'How absolutely lovely,' cried Frances, wide awake. 'But that will be wonderful. You'll enjoy that so much. How long is it since you've seen her?'

Hermione's mouth opened and then closed again.

Why did Frances always behave as if everything were simple and straightforward? How could she, Hermione, think about enjoying a visit from an old friend when there were so many important things to worry about?

'I shall have to sleep on the chaise longue,' she said in a martyred voice, 'and Freda will have to take my bed as it is the only one in the house.'

'Freda can have my little room. Then you can sleep in your own bed,' Frances suggested.

'Certainly not. She's my visitor. I want her to wake up in my house.'

'At half-past five?'

'Don't be silly, Frances. I can't tell her that there isn't room for her and push her next door. Not when she's come all that way.'

'I don't see why not. It seems perfectly sensible to me. She can have my little room to herself and join you when she's ready for the day's activities.'

'No, Frances. That won't do. I shall sleep on the chaise longue. I don't sleep anyway so it won't make any difference.'

Frances thought about the Victorian chaise longue with its prickly, horsehair mattress covering a multitude of arthritic joints and attachments and felt sorry for Freda. Sleeping on it wasn't going to transform Hermione's mood to the gaiety of a sea full of dolphins.

'Asked me to arrange a trip to Scotland. I've spent all morning ringing up the travel agents. They talked to me as if I were an imbecile. You can't just make arrangements for a trip to Scotland as if you were going to the market on the bus, you know,' Hermione pointed out severely.

In her inner ear Frances heard her mother's conversations with the travel agents. Hermione was saying that the early train started too early and the late one left too late, this bus took too long, that bus went too fast. No, they didn't want to pay all that, wasn't there something cheaper? Everything was so extortionate nowadays. It must have no pets and be facing the sea and could the travel agent guarantee, absolutely guarantee, that the beds would not be damp?

'Well, you can have a good holiday here. Go off for outings a day at a time. There are lots of places to take Freda to.' Frances had started the serious business of making the day's first pot of tea, not counting the one at half-past five with Albert.

'And she wants me to go to Exeter for a week to see her relations,' Hermione snorted.

'Marvellous. It'll be a nice holiday for both of you. You can explore Exeter together.'

It was no use talking to Frances. She simply didn't appreciate how difficult life was. She would go home and telephone Nigel. She'd have to tell him that he was meeting Freda's plane in Manchester at half-past six in the morning. Nigel would understand what a trial this visit was going to be.

Frances, now that she was awake, contemplated the intricacies of human behaviour, and the morning, as if in response to the command of Hermione's mood, took on a sulky expression. Yesterday's heat was sifting through the trees with little, protesting squeaks as the wind rose under a hot, heavy, rumbling parade of dark cloud.

Hermione, stepping out of her daughter's front door, was struck by the threat of storm. She hurried to her own front door, opened it, entered, then changed her mind.

She returned to the cottage next door.

'Frances, there's going to be a gale. Tie everything down.'

That was the answer. Why hadn't Frances thought of it before? Human complexities would all be unravelled if one could only achieve this feat. Tie everything down.

❦

31

Thelma decided that she must get a job.

Joan had managed very well over the years with her three cleaning jobs and her maintenance. So could she. The money left on the coffee table by Howard would pay the gas bill and keep them going for a short time but it would not solve the problem of how she was going to spend the rest of her life.

She was glad that Marcus had been found safely. Poor Alice must have been frantic. But she wished he could have chosen some other time to go missing. It might be weeks before Howard came again. She had been bitterly disappointed when she finished tidying the kitchen and discovered that he and the table lighter had disappeared.

Poor Howard. She found that she did not feel angry or jealous or hurt any more. Thinking about Howard merely filled her with pity and a kind of hopeless remorse. Why she should feel remorse she didn't know. She had always done her best to live up to the standards be set. She had tried to make up for the disasters of his childhood. She knew, however, that nobody could make Howard happy – that he was searching for what he already possessed but had failed to recognise and would spend his time drifting from one panorama to another without ever touching the stability of earth, as an uprooted clump of watercress drifts downstream, its trailing roots seeking the nourishment that the movement of the water constantly denies it.

Picking up the local paper she turned to the 'situations vacant' columns. There were three separate advertisements asking for people to wash up in pubs. She didn't think that would be the answer to the problem.

It would have to be a job which took place during school hours. Of course, Karen and Andrew could go to wait for her at Joan's or at Alice's if the times overlapped, or they could wait with Frances. They always enjoyed visits to Frances who, although she had no children of her own, had a way of finding interesting things for them to do when they were in her care.

Somebody wanted a nanny. No. She didn't think she would like to be a nanny. It would worry her too much, knowing that she was taking the place of the child's real mother.

There were two advertisements which asked for shorthand typists. Thelma had done a secretarial course when she left school. Agnes had been very proud of her. Next to being a teacher, being a secretary was a mark of social status which put you above mill, factory and shopworkers. But the only secretarial job she had ever taken had only lasted for six months. She could keep a house in order but papers she could not cope with. In spite of the secretarial course, any pressure would slide her into a kind of panic which slowed her down just when the office wanted her to be speeding up. No. She did not want to be a secretary again. Offices gave her a trapped feeling. It was in offices that you met men who put everything into slots. This included people. It was in offices that you met men like Howard.

There were one or two advertisements for factory jobs. She didn't think that she would last long in front of a machine. Machines gave her the same sort of feeling as offices. If you didn't persistently feed and tend them they turned on you with savagery.

There was one job which sounded hopeful. It offered thirty pounds a week for six hours' work. But it did not specify the nature of the work and Thelma knew from people who had applied for this sort of job that it would probably be more like thirty hours' work and six pounds in return and involve knocking on doors and waking people who had just come off the night shift and were not pleased to see you, let alone part with their hard-earned cash to buy whatever you were trying to sell them.

No, a cleaning job, like Joan's, would be the thing. But there were always plenty of energetic women to do other people's housework for them.

She put the paper down and sat deep in thought.

Thelma did not really want a job. She had always found plenty of work to do at home. There was the bread to make, the pickling and preserving, the cleaning, the garden to look after. Yet if she applied for social security and stayed at home to do these things as before she would have to make some sort of legal arrangement with Howard about maintenance which would put an official seal on their separation. She would rather remain dependent upon his goodwill and have a job in order to pay the mortgage and the bills than close the door and admit that her marriage was ended. She knew that Howard was not likely to let them starve or go to prison. And in any case, the idea of accepting money from the state, as if she were incapable of making her own way, did not appeal to her at all. Howard would have to pay for himself, she knew that. He wouldn't expect that woman to keep him. But she also knew that he would want to provide for her as well as he could. Money was very important to Howard. Giving money was one of the ways in which he felt able to give himself. It would just be a question of sorting out what was fair. And if she could find a job she would be in a better position to do that. She was enough like Jeremiah to feel that people should fend for themselves and she knew that he would have expected her to buckle-to in her present circumstances.

A shadow crossed the window. She went to the door and let her brother in.

The Mayor looked at Thelma and Thelma, determined not to cry, gave him a brave little smile.

'Nay,' said the Mayor, putting his big arms around her. 'Nay, lass. You deserve better than this.'

Seeing that she was going to be upset he pulled himself together and tiptoed across the gleaming linoleum. He always felt constrained to tiptoe in Thelma's house. You never knew what might break. But in his boots, and wearing his dungarees, it was difficult to tiptoe with dignity.

Thelma smiled a proper smile.

'Have I to take them off?' asked the Mayor, indicating his wellingtons and the wisps of straw and hen dirt they were distributing about the floor.

'Please yourself, Fred. I can easily mop it again,' Thelma assured him. She set about making some tea.

'Not for me,' the Mayor said hastily. 'I've come prepared.' He searched around in his many pockets until he located the diesel bottle.

Thelma sat down again.

'Now then,' the Mayor began, 'you'll come home to the farm and live with me.'

'That I will not,' said Thelma. But she added, 'No, I don't mean to sound sharp. It's good of you, Fred, and I do appreciate it. But this is my home now and because I've no husband is no reason to uproot the children from where they were born, unless there's no help for it.'

'How will you manage?' Fred asked.

'Well, Howard will give me some money and I'll have to find a job.'

The Mayor took a comforting pull at his fuel supply.

'I don't like to think of you having to go out to work, Thelma,' he said when he was fortified. 'It's not been done that way in our family for a time. What will you do?'

'I was just looking in the paper. There's not much choice.'

The Mayor's face took on an expression of deep concentration.

'There's your typing and that,' he suggested.

'No. I don't like offices.'

'What would you like?'

'Some cleaning. Or something out of doors.'

The Mayor sat bolt upright. His face cleared as if it had been a sky filled with seagulls swept by the beginnings of a gale force wind.

'That's it,' he crowed. 'That's it. Wey-hey. Wey-hey. That's it.'

'What's it?' Thelma asked, wondering whether he'd had a drop before he came.

'Joshua Lofthouse. Old Joshua Lofthouse. Eggs. Telling me one of his girls was pregnant. Not coming back after the babby. Doing it properly, I shouldn't wonder. Breast-feeding. Can't get somebody to do that for you, you see. At least, you can. But it's not done so much nowadays.'

'Lofthouse's Egg Packers?' Thelma suddenly felt a little trickle of something that was hard to explain running through the desert that her mind had become. Lofthouse's Egg Packers was situated just on the outskirts of the village, at the end of a long lane. She could walk there easily. It was a small enterprise, not many workers. It would make a lovely walk each day. And Joshua was reputed to be a good employer who looked after his people and paid them fairly.

'Met him in town, at the Golden Hind. Just came up in conversation, like.' The Mayor felt ebullient. He had said something to make Thelma happy. 'If that's what you'd like I'll give him a tinkle.' He'd never been able to resist doing what he could to make Thelma happy, ever since she was little. She was proud, he knew. But work was nothing to be ashamed of. Joshua would look after her.

'Yes,' said Thelma, trying not to show that she was hopeful. 'He may already have somebody. Jobs are hard to get.'

'Too far for anybody in town. Has to be locals. One way to find out.'

He went to the telephone and lifted the receiver. Then he put it down again and began to search for the book. Howard had arranged the telephone corner. The telephone clung to the wall like a piece of crustaceous marine life. But the pad with the pencil and the list of important numbers like the doctor, the hospital and the parson – though why Howard should consider the parson's number important the Mayor couldn't think – the pad was hidden on a shelf under the mink-covered stool which lurked below the telephone. The stool was so low that you could not actually sit down on it while you spoke, but had to kneel.

The Mayor found the telephone book with the pad under the top of the stool and looked up Joshua's number.

Joshua said he'd be glad to accommodate Thelma. It wasn't a taxing job and they were a happy little crowd. She wasn't allergic, was she? Only once he had taken on somebody who was allergic. Terrible rash she came out in. Affected her eyes, too. Feathers, Joshua thought.

The Mayor said, no, Thelma wasn't allergic and she had been brought up with hens, as Joshua knew.

Thelma beamed at the Mayor.

'Now, that's given me a better outlook,' she said.

The Mayor decided that this would be a good moment to mention the date loaf.

He spent the rest of the morning telling his sister about Hermione's childhood.

32

Nigel met Freda at Manchester airport at half-past six in the morning.

Freda was no longer a big girl. She was now a tough little old lady – dotty as George, pliable as a young willow twig, vague as a lamb, good-natured as a perpetual drunk. Although she had not seen Nigel since he was a very young man she recognised him at once.

'Hello there. Hello there, Nigel,' she cried across the air terminal, making towards him like a kingfisher on to its lunch.

She had spent so long saying goodbye to the lifelong friends she had made on the flight from Victoria that she was the last one to arrive in the now almost empty precinct and Nigel had begun to wonder whether Hermione, in her anxiety to get things right, had got things wrong, as she sometimes did.

Freda was smartly clad in a white raincoat cut in the

military style and appeared to be unencumbered by luggage. Her short grey hair, permed to resemble the fine culture which grows on top of a dish of rice that has been forgotten for a week or two, gleamed around her merry face. Though the same age as Hermione she appeared to be much younger, lean and athletic where Hermione was matronly and cumbersome.

After the first rapturous greetings there was a little pause in which Nigel expected Freda to make some sort of reference to her luggage. This did not happen.

'Well, Freda,' said Nigel, 'we must find your suitcases.'

'Oh, I don't think I had any suitcases,' said Freda. 'I haven't changed my clothes or anything you know, dear, I just slept in my seat. They tip them and you can lie back. Very comfortable. It's quite something looking out over the mountains.'

'But you've come for three weeks,' Nigel protested. 'You must have some luggage.'

'Waydaminute. Waydaminute. I did, too. I had a suitcase. Now I wonder what happened to that. I haven't seen it the whole way. Not the whole way.'

Nigel sat Freda down on a seat and went off to seach for her one suitcase.

When he returned with one large suitcase and two smaller ones Freda had vanished.

He found her again in the airport shop. She greeted him as if seeing him for the first time.

'I was just gonna get a taxi,' she explained. 'It was so good of you to come.'

As Hermione had predicted, Nigel could see that this visit was going to be full of incident.

33

❦

As she returned from buying pie and peas for tea Sharon realised that life with Howard was a drag.

She had met somebody who did not work in the office. His name was Bruce. On Saturday she had bought herself a new skirt. Bruce was the assistant manager of the boutique in which she was trying them on. The skirt she chose was lovely. But Bruce, who approached her to help in making the decision, was even lovelier.

'Now this purple one is in the latest style,' he said, draping it around himself and leaning slightly backwards like somebody being discouraged from taking the front of the queue by somebody else who was there already.

'They are all being worn like this in London,' he assured her. He spoke the words 'in London' as if uttering a spell, some kind of centuries-old pedigree, a total guarantee of the garment's total superiority.

'Oh yes. I saw one on telly,' Sharon agreed, thereby disclosing her credentials as a connoisseur of clothing.

The purple skirt fitted Sharon's delicate figure like a very fine chamois leather glove. Kid would not have clung so invitingly to a slim and elegant hand as the purple skirt clung to Sharon's thin, bony shape.

'Very, very fetching,' breathed the admiring Bruce.

'I'll take it,' said Sharon, in the sort of voice which indicated that if Bruce wished to display her in it she would not be averse. Bruce asked her what she would be doing on Saturday evening.

'Oh, nothing much. I lead a dull life,' said Sharon wistfully.

The following Saturday Bruce had taken her to a disco. She

had told Howard that she was going to visit her mother. The evening had been a great success, as had the purple skirt. Bruce had told her about his wife and three children. He had been thinking of leaving them for some time. Sharon's heart had been stirred by the tale of his domestic imprisonment, which slid into her experienced ear as though greatly relieved to find a suitable home.

Sharon didn't know why on earth she had ever asked Howard to come and live with her. He had always seemed attractive at the office. But around the house he was a source of constant irritation. He never seemed to be satisfied with anything. Also, he talked a great deal about his wife, Thelma, which Sharon found boring. It was one thing to listen to frustrated husbands when you were hoping for rewards for your apparent sympathy. It was quite another to have to listen to them along with the socks and the underpants and trying to think of things to buy which bad stomachs could assimilate.

She climbed the dingy staircase, her heart already filled with anticipation of a weekend at home with Bruce in her love nest. If she could get rid of Howard by then it might be this very weekend. With the breezy confidence of the utterly callous she knew that Howard would not be too difficult to get rid of.

'Pie and peas,' she announced, throwing her parcel on to the card table. Howard had set the table with the two stained knives and the two stained forks and two plates from the kitchenette which he had warmed with the reluctant assistance of the churlish water heater. He found that he was constantly hungry while living with Sharon, and almost as constantly in pain, either as a result of what she had given him to eat or from waiting for it to arrive.

'Couldn't we have something homemade, sometimes?' he asked plaintively.

Poor Howard. He did not know that the sword was dangling by a thread above him.

'I'm not working like a slave all day and coming home to start again, you know,' Sharon replied tartly. 'I'm not one of those women who hang around the house all day doing nothing and then rush about cooking at the last minute to try and make it look as if they've been busy. You had one of those and she didn't seem to suit you. Now you're grumbling because I'm not like her.' Sharon knew that this outburst was akin to amputating the finger to repair a broken fingernail, but Howard's complaint fitted into her plans very well. She would certainly amputate.

'No, of course not. I'm not suggesting that you should. It's just that some things, like omelettes, are very easy to make and nice, sometimes. For a change,' he added lamely.

'Then make your own bloody omelette,' Sharon suggested hospitably.

'I didn't mean right now.' Howard was beginning to feel the faintest awareness that something heavy and sharp was moving about in the air over his head.

'Then what did you mean? You're always on at me. You don't like my flat. You don't like the food I eat. The only thing you like about me is having a good poke. Well, I'm not short of people who like more about me than that, you know.' Sharon found that shouting at Howard was doing her good.

'Now look, Sharon.' Howard's stomach felt as if it was being ripped and pulled out between his ribs at the back in two pieces. 'Now look, dear. There's no need to get so angry.' He began to cut up his pie and force it into his mouth with the tepid peas, trying to look as if this was an enjoyable experience. His mind, like the leading horse which raised a cheer from the betting shop below, was running far ahead of events. If he could get her on to the bed all would be well. Once he had undressed her everything would be all right. She was just feeling tense. There had been a lot of pressure at the office about the location of the new public conveniences. Sharon had been given the job of sorting out various petitions which had been handed in objecting to the plan to situate them next to the fountain. Why the townspeople couldn't mind their own business and leave things to the experts, Howard would never know.

He smiled at her. He smiled his special, knowing smile.

'And you needn't make sheep's eyes at me. I've got a headache. And my feet hurt,' Sharon said.

Howard carried the plates into the kitchenette.

'Perhaps it's your shoes,' he suggested, looking at the heels which jutted from the straps around Sharon's almost bare feet like crucifixion nails.

'And what's wrong with my shoes?' Sharon saw Bruce bending over her. In his haste to have his way with her he ripped her blouse. He could always replace it from the boutique. 'These are my best sandals. They cost me twenty-nine pounds thirty, and that was in the sale.'

Howard felt the stir of air caused by the swinging of the sword. His stomach was now being drawn downwards by its unwelcome contents, sinking with groans and gurgles and little cries of distress into the maelstrom of his gut.

At this stage he could see that he and Sharon were going to have a disagreement. A ray of hope fluttered on and off in his shady mind like a faulty fluorescent light.

'Sharon, dear,' he said with his knowing smile, 'we are having our first quarrel, aren't we?'

'First and last.' Sharon was triumphant. It had all been a piece of cake. 'I'm sick of you draping yourself around my place like wet seaweed. Go home to your Thelma. You're always telling me how wonderful she is. Go back to the outback where you belong. I'm a sophisticated woman. What you want is a lump of lard.'

Howard was stunned. Was he right in thinking Sharon had implied he was not a man of the world? Surely not. Visions of his earlier conquests trailed through his consciousness. All of these encounters had ended when *he* decided that he would end them. None of his other women had ever shown any dissatisfaction. Howard was stricken.

He tried again.

'Now, come on, dear. You know you don't mean that. You're just tired. Let me massage your back.'

'Tired I am. Tired of you.' Sharon snipped the thread and the sword fell neatly through the top of Howard's incredulous skull. 'And I've met a proper fella. So move on.'

Howard sat down on the edge of the bed. He had been trying to manoeuvre her towards it, still thinking, in the death throes of his stomach and the last flutterings of his passion, that once he had divested her of her clothing everything would be all right.

He could see that events were getting out of control.

Suddenly the revolution in his abdomen, too, was out of control.

He ran to the bathroom and disgorged his pie and peas into the lavatory. When he flushed it he noticed, as he had noticed every time he'd used it, that the ballcock was not working properly. He felt a great sense of relief. He could stop thinking that he would have to mend the lavatory now. It was no longer his concern.

As he took his suitcase and trailed down the dismal corridor he began to make a list in his mind of all the things he would not now have to think about mending.

Halfway down the staircase leading to the front door with its detached eyeball he turned and climbed back up again. Ignoring Sharon who was ostentatiously applying lipstick to her abundant lips he took the onyx table lighter from its position in solitary splendour at the centre of the card table. With its departure the only trace of elegance flickered and went out of Sharon's home.

After all, it was his.

He had not yet begun to think about how he was going to approach Thelma. He must give his stomach and his self-esteem time to adjust.

❦

34

Since Howard left home Thelma had not been able to feel the joy of the summer in which everyone she met, except Aunt Ella who thought it was too hot, seemed to be rejoicing. But as she walked down the lane to Joshua Lofthouse's Egg Packing Firm she began to notice the faintest whispers of happiness in the ruffling of the giant leaves on the chestnut trees and the soft tearing sounds of the sheep stuffing themselves oblivious with grass.

In the sewage works a green metal rectangular container was being filled noisily with waves of water like an absent-minded landing craft on the beach which had drunk the sea instead of swimming in it. She hurried past as everyone always hurried past the sewage works but she noticed that it was not as redolent as it usually seemed to be. Perhaps the hawthorn hedge which always did its best to perfume the air with a more appropriate scent was winning.

The school term did not start for another three days but Frances was going to look after the children until then. She had refused to let Thelma pay her for this service, insisting that it was a privilege to have children entrusted to one, but Thelma had secretly determined to wait until they went back to school and then buy Frances a nice present with part of her first wage.

The lane wandered downhill towards the next mill town with its black diamond pattern of terraces and factories and mills crouching lazily under the hot sun, like a tropical frog.

Approaching the reservoir she turned left up a private lane which led to the shambling farm in whose outbuildings the egg-packing took place. She stopped outside the gate of the yard, prudently eyeing two large Alsatian dogs, which barked agreeably and wagged their vigilant tails but did not look as if they would admit her to their territory without some sort of introduction. A young lad, hearing the barking, came out of a shed from which turkeys were craning their necks to see what the uproar was about.

'I'm Thelma Heyworth,' said Thelma. 'I've come to start work today.'

'Belt up, Laddie. Belt up, King,' said the boy. 'Pay no attention to them. I'll shut them up for now but they're soft as babies when they get to know you.' He nodded and smiled at Thelma, who watched the dogs leave the gateway reluctantly and follow the lad around to the back of the turkey house.

The lad returned.

'I'm Geoff,' he said. 'I'll take you to May and June.'

It did not seem to strike him that he had said anything that might sound odd to a newcomer so Thelma did not echo the query in her mind. She walked across the cobbled yard behind him. He pulled back a sliding door and made an elaborate bow to Thelma from just inside the building.

'May and June,' he announced ceremoniously.

'Oh, thank you,' said Thelma, going in.

It was cooler in the small whitewashed outhouse. Empty and full cartons lined the walls almost to the ceiling. Egg trays, filled with an assortment of eggs: very small, humble eggs, huge, bossy eggs, pale, apologetic eggs, eggs with no particular character which just sat and looked decorative and dark brown eggs which looked as if they had recently returned from a holiday on the African coast, rose layer on layer in front of the cartons. Bales of empty egg trays tied up with coarse string stood about waiting to get on with the job. There was barely room to move.

It reminded Thelma of her childhood. Not the eggs and the work to be done but the ordered, clean, stone building, the faint farm smells, the feeling of permanence. She put out her hand and touched the smooth cardboard of one of the cartons.

A message of happiness came through the ends of her

fingers and rushed into her veins. This was going to be a good place for her.

'No need to test the cartons, they're all grade one,' said May, laughing as she struggled into her overall. She offered her hand to Thelma. It was a warm, friendly, welcoming, motherly hand. Thelma was very sensitive to the feel of hands. You could tell a lot about people by the way they shook hands. May was going to look after her.

'And I'm June,' said June, 'and it isn't a joke. I was born in June and she was born in May so that's how we were both christened by our respective parents. Fate has brought us together,' she added, throwing her arms around May and giving her solid frame a hug.

Thelma looked at June.

'June Rawsthorne?' she asked hesitantly.

'Not any more. June Heaton for the last twelve years.' She unwrapped her arms from May and approached Thelma with a look of sudden recognition. 'I know you, don't I? Thelma. Thelma Pickles from Yardale Farm.'

Thelma's cup of consolation was full.

'Rotten sod. Always got your needlework right. Do you remember when we made blouses in the second form? I cut a hole in the collar of mine and had to patch it before it was even finished. "You've spoiled it, of course, my girl, but it will remind you to keep your mind on what you are doing in future,"' said June, in the tones of a refined spinster school-marm.

'Miss Pinder,' Thelma observed. 'She knew all about the posh way of doing things but my mum was better at patchwork, and my grandmother.'

It was half-past eight.

'Come on, ladies. We've a shed full of eggs to sort. Time we made a start,' said May.

In the centre of the room was an ancient but effective-looking machine. This machine rolled the eggs into a scale, weighed them and sent them out along channels across a large tray graded according to size ready to be packed in their respective boxes and then in the big cardboard cartons.

June showed Thelma how to inspect the eggs to make sure

that no damaged or very dirty ones went into the machine, keeping them travelling down the metal, cotton-reel-shaped rollers to the scale so that the tray always had eggs in it for May to put into the appropriate boxes at the other side. If an egg was cracked or misshapen it had to be put in a special egg tray. These eggs were sent to the bakeries.

'We don't waste any of them,' May explained. 'Even the ones we drop, and they're all guaranteed to break, you know. We save as much as we can and Joshua's wife beats them up and freezes them.'

Thelma began to work. She was conscious that she had to make several decisions in a short space of time if she were to keep the rollers filled. She had to decide whether an egg was clean enough or needed a wipe with the wet sponge. She had to decide whether it was too dirty and must be rejected altogether, whether it had any almost invisible cracks, was too deformed or whether its shell was too thin. She concentrated very hard. She did not want to drop one. When June was demonstrating she had held four eggs in her hands at a time. Thelma knew it would be a long time before she could achieve this.

But she had always possessed what employers choose to call manual skill. Soon she became more relaxed. She told them about Karen and Andrew and, eventually, about Howard. She heard in return about May's husband Clifford who had suffered a stroke but was still a bad bugger and June's twin girls, whom nobody could ever tell apart.

As it grew hotter June opened the sliding door and the chuntering of hens and turkeys sieved through farmyard smells and the exploratory paddings in and out of the two Alsatians dripped into their sanctuary as from a slab of sunlight. A turkey which had strayed from its confines poked his pale neck inside.

'Be off with you. You're no use to us,' scolded May. 'Reminds me of an unfortunate accident that befell a friend of mine, Mavis Broughton. Works as a typist at Michelin's.' She stacked three egg boxes on the table behind her. They were whisked away by June. 'Mavis and her husband Alec, a coalminer, jolly sort of man, went out for a meal just before

Christmas with their friends Emmanuel and Sandra Scholes. She's a hairdresser. He has a building business. Well, they went out, as I say, for a meal at that pub at Oldchapel.'

'Went to a wedding reception there once. Beautiful buffet,' June said.

'Yes. They had a good meal and they'd all had a bit to drink. Quite a bit to drink, in fact. Were all feeling happy, what you might call festive, you know, in the Christmas mood. Well, they decided to go back to Sandra and Manny's at the end of the evening for some coffee. When they arrived there, Alec fell asleep at the bottom of the stairs and Mavis went up to the bathroom to pay a visit.

'While she was gone Manny and Sandra decided to have a bit of fun with her. On the kitchen table was their turkey, thawing ready for the oven. So they took its neck and placed it between the sleeping Alec's legs. Then they went back to make the coffee.

'A few minutes later they heard a bloodcurdling scream from Mavis. They sauntered out to the hall, prepared to be all innocent-like and there was Mavis at the top of the stairs, and Alec at the bottom, and the turkey neck still in place. But the cat was eating it.'

Thelma dropped her first egg.

Overcome with the story, confusion and dismay about the egg and the fact that the rollers were still passing, empty, she scooped up its broken shell and began to apologise as if she had shattered the whole beautiful, busy morning.

June was choking.

'I think that's a terrible story,' she gasped, wiping her eyes.

Thelma continued to apologise.

'Don't be a dozy pillock,' said May comfortably, 'you're initiated now, that's all.'

Now Thelma liked a joke as much as anyone. She laughed with May and June. But at the back of her mind a lingering doubt about this story of May's lurked for some time. Thelma had a strong, literal mind.

Surely, she thought, surely, even though they were all a bit happy, Mavis must have known that Alec would have felt it, asleep though he was.

At lunchtime they sat on bales of egg trays to eat their sandwiches.

'Now you forget about your troubles and enjoy life,' May advised Thelma. 'You're among friends here. No need for any side. If you feel like screaming of a morning, have a good scream. Then we'll all settle down for a laugh. Nothing like a laugh.'

And indeed, May's deep chuckles and June's staccato shrieks punctuating the hours came to epitomise Thelma's new situation as a working woman, filling the fertile ovary of the outhouse with stories of times gone by, views about life which struck Thelma as being very original and daring, and heartfelt communications of kindness and understanding as they sorted, graded and packed, reminiscing with active, testing hands through the fragrant day.

The smooth, firm, solid eggs had taken Thelma over, soothed her aching and despair, re-established her youthful sense of the wholesomeness of creation, had taken her back, without allowing her the sadness of regression, to the days when what her hands had done gave her all the satisfaction she could wish for. So she inspected, wiped, sorted and admired the eggs and watched them trundling away on the metal cotton reels to be weighed, with the pride of a hen.

35

'Did you know that here in England unemployment has reached over three million? Isn't that dreadful. What do they do?' asked Freda, reading an old newspaper for the sixteenth time since her arrival.

Freda loved English newspapers. There was something about them. Not the news. She would have enjoyed them however old they were. Hermione, in the role of poor pensioner, never bought any. If there was something that she particularly wanted to see she would wait until William was at home and ask him if she could borrow the relevant copy, which was sure to be somewhere around as Frances always forgot to throw them away. In the absence of newsprint for Freda to read at Hermione's house, Frances had taken in a large pile of old newspapers, some of them almost reaching antiquity.

'You've read me that bit seven times this morning already, and once or twice yesterday,' Hermione commented, wearing the expression of a parent listening to its ungifted child practising on the violin.

When they were not out on an expedition Freda would sit and entertain herself, and attempt to entertain Hermione, by reading out extracts from these yellowed journals. Hermione tolerated a certain number of repetitions and then indulged in an explosion, sometimes only a small splutter, as of the gas failing to light the first time, sometimes more in the nature of a little Hiroshima.

'Really,' she complained to Frances, 'she has no memory at all. Absolutely none. I don't think she should ever have travelled so far alone.'

However, Freda's memory was only partially disabled. She could remember in detail how they had managed to resuscitate the exterminated piano and a great many other achievements which Hermione had forgotten. These memories afforded both the old ladies a great deal of enjoyment. Frances worried in case the disappointment of finding that Freda's visit was a success would cause Hermione to have a personality crisis.

Today they were going to the market.

'Oh, I adore English markets,' Freda had exclaimed when Frances suggested it. 'Will there be a stall which sells wool? I want some with bobbles in it. You can't get it anywhere in Canada, you know. Not anywhere.'

First they went to the bank. After a long friendly conversation with the young cashier in which Freda informed the whole queue of customers and all those behind the grill, somewhat unnecessarily, that she came from the other side, she eventually emerged clutching a bundle of notes which amounted to one hundred and seventy-five pounds.

'Do you think this will be enough? Whaddya think?' she asked Hermione, waving the haystack of money about under her friend's inherited nose.

'Good heavens, Freda. Of course it will be enough.' Hermione was shocked.

'Better put it in your wallet,' Frances suggested, wondering whether any mugger would take on three females, two elderly and one middle-aged, if one of them looked as fierce as Hermione looked.

They had only been in the market hall for five minutes when Freda got lost.

Frances tried to stay calm. It was a long way to the airport. Freda would be unlikely to set off for another continent.

'You go up this aisle and I'll go up the next one. We'll meet at the top,' she instructed her furious mother.

In this manner they combed the whole market hall without uncovering any trace of their missing visitor. They progressed to the stalls of the open market.

At the far end of the open market Frances spotted a white macintosh cut in the military style. But she dismissed it at once. Freda had not been wearing a hat. Then she allowed the white macintosh back into her consideration and hurried towards it.

Perched on the top of Freda's grey frizzy head was a magnificent puce edifice. Freda was not so much wearing the hat as carrying it on the crown of her skull in the manner of an African woman carrying a vessel of water.

'Oh, that's lovely,' said Frances, out of breath and referring more to having found Freda than anything else. Freda was rummaging in her shopping bag.

'You like it, huh? I bought it. I found the wool, too.' She indicated mountains of wool on the stall beside her. 'I spent twenty-five pounds on wool. But I don't seem to have any money.' She continued to open and close the six purses which had emerged from the depths of her shopping bag.

The owner of the wool stall, with three large brown paper bags full of wool in her arms, stood tolerant but watchful. She was not going to let this transatlantic sale slip away if she could help it.

Hermione arrived, harassed and breathing heavily.

'We've looked everywhere,' she said accusingly to Freda. 'Where on earth have you been?'

'Oh, I've just been wandering around. D'ya like the hat?'

'We can't find her money,' said Frances, opening and closing the six purses for the third time. In the heat of the market she was beginning to feel cold, anticipating questions at the police station. What had the lady been doing with so much money lying about loose in an open shopping bag?

'Waydaminute. Waydaminute.' Freda's memory clicked on. 'I didn't put it in any of those. I just pushed it in here.'

Down one side of her shopping bag was a large unfastened pocket. Sticking out of the top of this pocket, like an invitation to a banquet, was Freda's one hundred and seventy-five pounds.

'I paid for the hat with one of these,' said Freda, brandishing a twenty-pound note, 'and the woman gave me some of these back,' brandishing three five-pound notes, 'and I just put them all in with the others.'

Still holding the brown paper bags full of wool the owner of the stall smiled with pleasure.

Hermione seethed.

'Really, Freda, you don't know how lucky you are,' she expostulated. 'For goodness sake, put it away. Somebody could have stolen all that and you wouldn't have known anything about it.'

'You're right. I wouldn't.' Freda giggled. 'Old sheep's brain.'

They sorted it all out, paying for Freda's wool and putting her fortune safely under one of the brown paper bags in the shopping bag and thanking the stallholder warmly as if she had been responsible for all this happiness.

'How are you going to take this home to Canada?' Frances asked, her arms full of parcels of wool with bobbles in it.

'Oh, I guess I'll just send it by post,' Freda replied comfortably.

Hermione looked more cheerful. If there was one thing she enjoyed it was making up packages for the post. They needn't go anywhere else today. This would occupy the rest of the afternoon, if they managed to get Freda home safely.

They managed to get Freda home safely and Frances found that the puce hat was perched on top of Freda's head because it still contained its tissue paper stuffing. She began, discreetly, to remove it.

'No, don't do that, dear.' Freda fell on her like a cormorant upon a fish. 'I'm leaving it in. Make it easier to put in my suitcase for going home.'

So for three weeks Freda wore the hat, commanding and erect on the top of her head like a giant aubergine, thereby causing a great deal of innocent merriment.

36

They were all lying about on Alice's half of the patio, the children limp and grubby, wanting something to do but not having the energy to think of anything. The sun stared down accusingly. A giant poppy in a tub sat there looking smug, like someone who has finished the housework and is sitting in a deckchair while the rest of the world is going frantic with a duster.

'Well, I'd like to go for a picnic.' Hadrian had lined up the Trojan fleet along the top of the wall. But without water it was not progressing.

'Or build a secret den,' Endymion added.

'We can't build a secret den because it wouldn't be secret.' Karen had Howard's precise turn of mind.

'It would be secret for a lot of people. We would be the only ones who knew about it.' Hadrian made a hurricane with a sweep of his hand and the Trojan fleet was navigated over the wall and fell to the lawn below. Hadrian leaned over the wall and looked down at his ships.

'It would depend on where we built it, how many people knew about the secret,' said Endymion. 'If we went right up the stream nobody would know but us.'

They all turned and looked at Marcus who was sitting on the top step lost in thought. He didn't notice their interest in him.

'It's because of the stream and Marcus the Maggot that we have to tell everybody everything,' Endymion added.

'My mum says if I ever go missing like that I needn't bother to come home because she'll wallop me until the seat drops out of my pants,' said Martin ruefully.

Alice had been working on an article about the symbolism in *Antony and Cleopatra*. Her mind was filled with poetry. She wound her long plait around her head and murmured, 'Give me my robe. Put on my crown . . .'

Frances, more conscious of the presence of actual children wanting to be entertained, was drawing a picture of Toad for Andrew who was leaning over the paper watching so closely that his nose was inhibiting the drawing's execution.

The three small rabbits were chewing grass on the edge of the lawn while Toad crouched reluctantly for his portrait, held down by Karen.

'We could take the rabbits down to the wood and give them a picnic,' she suggested, stroking Toad's resistant backside.

'Don't be silly. They'd all go off and become wild rabbits. Then the wood would be full of half white and half brown rabbits and Tom'd be shooting Toad's grandchildren.' Endymion didn't want anything to do with genocide.

'How about staying here and having a nice game in the garden,' said Alice, thinking that if the children were safely occupied at home she could go back to her article. Ideas were growing and blossoming in her mind like those Japanese paper flowers that you drop into a glass of water. Her immortal longings were battling with the certainty that if any of the children got into mischief David would be very difficult to pacify. They had been lucky last time. There could be something worse. And she couldn't let Frances look after them all.

'What are the other children doing?' asked Frances. If there had been a project they could simply have joined in.

'Nobody's doing anything. It's too hot. And there's nothing to do in the garden.' Endymion was lying along the top of the wall, his legs dangling over the sides like thin garments spread out to dry.

'If there was a tram we could go for a tram ride.' Marcus had been considering.

'The trams never came as far as this, even when there were trams.' Hadrian would have liked a tram ride, too.

'The Mayor says if there were some trams he could leave his tractor at home. He has to go everywhere on his tractor,' said Endymion.

'How about a walk up to see the Mayor?' asked Frances. 'He might have something to look at, some baby pigs, or a calf.'

'Yes, let's go and see the Mayor.' Marcus made their minds up.

There was a general stir.

Alice thought this was a good idea. She could walk slowly with Frances at the back and think about Cleopatra. It was quite a long walk to Yardale Farm. It would take them half an hour to get there.

'Uncle Fred's cat Flora is just ready to have kittens,' Andrew volunteered. The drawing was finished and Karen had taken Toad back to his mansion.

The kittens were the deciding factor.

They trailed off up the hill like pilgrims on their way to a distant shrine.

What they could not have guessed was that Hermione and Freda had made the journey before them and were already comfortably settled in the cool recesses of the farm parlour being lavishly entertained by an ecstatic Fred Pickles.

37

✿

They had not caught him unawares. The date loaf was in a
cake tin on the kitchen table.

But he hadn't been expecting two of them.

Padding down the flagged corridor behind them in his
socks, the Mayor noticed that Mrs Tattersall's friend, Freda,
was only a little'un. She didn't have the same corporeal
advantages that Mrs Tattersall had. In fact, looking at her
critically from behind he decided that she didn't have any
corporeal advantages at all. You'd hardly know she had a
bum. The pale blue flowered cotton dress fell straight from
her thin shoulders to the backs of her thin brown knees.

Not that he was complaining. It made Mrs Tattersall seem
all the more inviting by comparison. She was wearing the
pink frock again. And having the lady from Canada, Freda,
made it better for the first visit. They would all be more at
their ease.

'First door on the left, ladies,' he called down the passage,
and Hermione obediently opened the parlour door and
stepped inside.

From the centre of the far wall a huge stone fireplace
presided over the room like a wise old judge over his court.
On either side of it bookshelves rose from the stone flags of
the floor to the oak beams of the ceiling.

Hermione stood transfixed. A farm cottage filled with
books.

'My old dad, Jeremiah, he was a great reader,' said the
Mayor apologetically. 'I'll just put a match to the fire. It's all
laid ready. Now, sit you down. I'll make a pot of tea.' He

crossed the room, lit the fire and shambled through a door in the corner to the kitchen.

'My goodness,' exclaimed Freda. 'My goodness. A real old English farmhouse. Look at the cute windows. And just look at the beautiful old furniture.'

Hermione, who had been stunned into a brief period of uncritical admiration, astonished by the sight of the rows and rows of languid books, turned her attention to the rest of the room.

There were two big, squashed armchairs by the fire, the pretty floral patterns on their covers just visible after multitudinous washings, and a big squashed sofa to match. The rest of the room was taken up by a gleaming mahogany sideboard of the Victorian era, over whose top an ornate mirror glowed pale as a studious forehead, a much older oak corner cupboard, an oak lowboy and a highly polished round mahogany table of the same vintage as the sideboard on a massive base which looked as if it were uttering a hoarse challenge to anybody who might be thinking of moving it an inch or two. There was also a more delicate china cabinet containing a tea set of great age over whose fragile surfaces an army of tiny flowers was staging a riot.

'Well, would you believe it?' Hermione sat down on the edge of one of the squashed armchairs by the fire which was already beginning to send reflections scuttering along all the dark wood surfaces in the room, like celebratory mice.

Freda sat down less cautiously on the squashed sofa and disappeared into the depths of its cushions so that the Mayor, emerging from the kitchen with a big brown pot of tea, three plain white cups and saucers and the date loaf on a tray, had a moment's anxiety when he couldn't immediately locate her.

He had intended to remove the dead rats from the wall of the backyard before Hermione came and it had slipped his memory. He didn't want them to wander out there before he had been out and seen to it.

'You've got a lovely place here, Mr Mayor,' cried Freda enthusiastically from the cushions. 'A real lovely old farmhouse.'

'Lovely,' echoed Hermione, recovering her composure.

The Mayor put the tray down on the massively rooted table and mopped his brow with his handkerchief.

'Been Pickles's in this house a long time,' he said. 'Reckon I shall be the last. My mother's crockery, though, in that cupboard. Came from her grandmother. Lived in Wales.' He began to pour tea into the three cups.

Hermione consulted her watch. It was only a quarter to three.

'No tea for me, thank you, Mr Pickles,' she said firmly.

'Oh, but I'll have some,' Freda interrupted hurriedly. The cushions, filled with generations of feathers, were sucking her further and further down.

The Mayor's face assumed a look of great concern.

'No tea, Mrs Tattersall?' he asked. 'No tea?'

Then a look of hope replaced his look of concern.

'You wouldn't prefer a drop of whisky?'

'Oh, I'll have some whisky, after my tea,' Freda assured him, close to the floor.

'But what will you have, my dear?' The Mayor despaired to think that Hermione had walked all this way and was not going to allow him to refresh her. 'You must have a piece of our Thelma's date loaf. It's the finest date loaf in Lancashire.'

'I'd like a piece of your sister's date loaf,' Hermione assented graciously.

Relieved, the Mayor cut the cake and turned his back on the ladies so that they would not notice his addition of diesel to his own cup before he passed the tea.

He felt in need of it. A man had to be in full possession of himself for occasions of this magnitude.

It was when Hermione, declaring the date loaf to be the best she had ever encountered, was enjoying her third slice, to the unspeakable joy of her host, and Freda and the Mayor were drinking diesel out of the kitchen mugs that the second group of pilgrims arrived at their destination.

'Drat it,' muttered the Mayor under his breath after he had answered the front door to his nephew and niece and the rest of the entourage.

'Has Flora had her kittens yet?' asked Karen, pushing past her uncle. 'Can we go and see?'

Within seconds all the romantic promise had faded from the Mayor's horizon as the rainbow fades from an enchanted landscape when the rain plummets down.

38

William had come home early. Although he had never wanted any children of his own he liked them and enjoyed their company, for short intervals. He knew that Frances was looking after Thelma's two for the last days of the holiday and he had thought that he would give her a surprise and help her to entertain them.

The front door was locked and when he walked into the cool house out of the sunlight he knew at once that she wasn't there. She often locked the door to keep Hermione at bay. But he knew that she was out because the house was quite different when she wasn't there. It wasn't that she made much noise. It wasn't that she usually sprang to greet him when he entered. It was just that without her the house looked neglected. When she was there her presence made it seem comfortable and loved.

He put his briefcase in the sitting room and went out to see if his mother-in-law would offer him a glass of sherry. Although it was early, he thought a glass of sherry might be in order. And Hermione might know where Frances was.

Hermione's door was locked too.

He returned home and made himself a cup of China tea.

Frances didn't care for China tea so he had his own little jar of it. George hadn't cared for China tea, either. But Hermione liked it. So for fifty years George and Hermione had drunk a mixture of China tea and Indian tea, which neither of them liked. This seemed to Hermione the sort of just and fair compromise which marriage demanded of married people.

William took his tea out into the garden and sat on a bench to admire his creation. It was his garden. Frances liked to fill the house with flowers and leave them there in vases for ever, declaring that they were even more beautiful when they were dead. But she didn't take any part in their production. It was his job to dig, hoe, riddle, plant and water.

She had once grown tomatoes. She had talked to them and looked after them with astonishing care. When they were ripe on the luxuriant plants, though, she had not allowed them to be eaten, explaining that she had watched them day by day enjoying their life and to eat them would amount to cannibalism. So they hung, brilliant against the pale, withering leaves until they dropped, lifeless, on to the soil at the top of the pots. Still Frances had been unable to pronounce them finished. So in the end, to save her grief, he had tipped them on to the compost heap. In the same way, a marrow which she had grown – dark green as the depths of the ocean with molten golden stripes – had become so hard that it couldn't be cut with a knife by the time he persuaded her it should be cooked.

Fortunately she did not have these feelings about all vegetables, only about the ones that she had grown herself.

But to be on the safe side and guard himself against unrewarded toil William restricted his garden to flowers and shrubs.

It was early and the sun was still high, but it had reached the other side of the house so his bench was in the shade. As he sat he thought about Frances and their marriage. Like all marriages it had been both a success and a disaster, depending on which way you looked at it. Most of the time he regarded it favourably. He didn't mind the mess and confusion. His working life provided him with order and routine. He didn't mind her absent-mindedness and her lack of wifely concern. These gave him a sense of freedom. He didn't mind her relationship with Albert. It made him happy that she was happy.

William, as well as being conventional and proper, had a wild streak, and this made him generous. William was not in love with a multitude of exotic women, or even with one exotic woman. He was not in love with money, which meant very little to him. He did not trail about to racecourses, or football grounds, or cricket pitches. He wasn't anxious to be learned. He didn't even collect anything.

William was in love with steam engines.

Women were like engines, he reflected. Engines were unique. There were no two engines with the same habits and the same way of going about things. In one engine a thick fire with a strong draught would burn like a dream while in another it would go out. Some women needed excitement to get up steam. Others needed quiet care and attention. Frances was one of these. Now the trouble with Hermione was that she couldn't read the signals. She never knew whether the arm was up or down. And her brakes were faulty. Whereas most people proceeded in the knowledge that the steam would drop sometime and the brakes go on, Hermione gathered speed and blew off constantly. You knew for certain that if you crossed her track you would be obliterated.

He sat and admired his sweetpeas. They had been magnificent this year. Climbing in intoxicating clusters up the trellis he had made for them they filled the centre of the garden, hanging in the air like a cloud of steam over a well-polished station with a neatly swept platform and little beds of petunias enclosed by whitewashed stones. Of course, this was a fantasy. His own garden did not resemble a railway station at all, except in its neatness and order. But his sweetpeas were most certainly as lovely as a cloud of steam from the Hardwick engine.

William leaned back against the wall of the house and felt the contentment of middle age. He had not set out to achieve much but he had achieved more than he had hoped for. He had not made too many demands but he had been given more than he had asked for. He had not looked for perfection, but many things, like driving and firing during his trips to Lakeside, had been perfect. He had never consciously invested everything in a human relationship yet to his married state he gave his innocent loyalty and from his married state he received a happy sense of stability, chaotic though its physical purlieus might be. His wife loved him dearly and he loved her. They both knew both of these things. Nothing else was relevant to their collective consciousness.

Into his relaxed mind as he leaned against the warm stone ran endless trains, hissing, coal-fed creatures drawing themselves together like well-fed cats about to spring. Trains were so satisfying. He chuckled, thinking of the shunting waggons that had fallen two hundred feet into an old mineworking at Lindal. The good people had filled in the hole and left them there. In generations to come, what would space-age archaeologists make of this strange phenomenon? Thinking that all progress was relative and that basic inventions were more thrilling than highly complex ones he shut his eyes. He could still see the bright metallic blue of the lobelias which the shade had not yet reached and the blaze of orange and dark red antirrhinums which glowed like a well-stoked engine fire. He could still see the glossy velvets of the pansies like wealthy passengers alighting and the excitement of his sweetpeas, a great cloud of steam.

39

Thelma saw it as she opened the door of her house, unwound the cotton square which she used to keep the hair out of her eyes while she worked and put down the shopping bag

in which she carried her sandwiches and her purse to Joshua
Lofthouse's Egg Packing firm. Howard's suitcase was standing in the hallway. It looked beaten.

She stood quite still. What was she going to do now?

Thelma had never regarded herself as an independent
woman. Capable, yes. But she was not one of those women
who, regarding themselves enslaved and demeaned by marriage, long to prove that they can manage perfectly well, if
not better, without it. Still, working at Joshua's egg-packing
had given her feelings of pride and satisfaction. She could
work, run her home and look after her children. She had
proved it.

Could she, though, work, run her home, look after her
children and cope with Howard? Coping with Howard was a
greater challenge than the other three put together.

She sighed.

'Thelma?' Howard's plaintive voice issued from his fringed
moquette armchair.

'I'm coming.' She shook out her brown curls and took off
her egg-packing overall which she had worn home because it
needed to be washed. Hanging it up she looked at her
reflection in the small mirror at the centre of the oak hall
stand with its metal slats for umbrellas and the little bench
under whose seat the children's wellies were kept. This was
the only piece of furniture she had been allowed by Howard
to accept among the many objects offered to her from the
farm by Agnes, and she had polished it lovingly over the years
with real beeswax until it glowed like a young chestnut when
you peel off the prickly green outer shell.

Her reflection expressed some of the happiness she had
been feeling before Howard's suitcase had intruded on her
mood and she adjusted it to disguise traces of uncertainty
introduced by this harbinger of yet another change.

'Where have you been? I've been waiting for half an hour.'

Howard had spent two nights at a bed and breakfast
establishment and when he had recovered from Sharon's
death blow suddenly became impatient to rid himself of his
memories of her, foremost among them his crabs.

'I didn't hurry home. I enjoy the walk,' she replied. 'I

suppose you want some tea.'

'Look, Thelma, I've got trouble,' said Howard, knowing that with his wife, the direct approach, if it involved action, was the best.

Thelma stopped on her way towards the kitchen. If that girl was pregnant, she was not going to bring up the baby. It would be just like Howard to assume that she would.

'What sort of trouble?' She was going to be quite ruthless about this. Quite ruthless. No baby.

Howard couldn't decide where to begin now that the moment had arrived. He had over-rehearsed during the past two days. Now, facile and too familiar, his lines had become confused. He began, accidentally, with his peroration. Instead of telling Thelma that he loved her, that he had been ill ever since he left home, that Sharon was a heartless bitch who lived like a pig, that she had described their intimate moments together to all the other girls in the office so that whenever he walked through the typing pool there was a gathering swell of giggling, he found himself saying,

'I've got crabs.'

Thelma's imagination failed. Had he been to the seaside?

'What do you mean, you've got crabs?'

Howard blushed. He scratched vigorously, partly by way of a straightforward demonstration, partly to stop the awful itching.

'Bugs. I've caught them from her.'

'Well, get up off the furniture then. Go on, out in the garden. Take your trousers and your underpants off. No, Howard, not here. Take them off outside. We'll burn them. Wait a minute, I'll get you a rug. No, you'd better just sit in the greenhouse. Nobody'll see you. Don't come into the house while I'm gone. I shan't be long.'

Thelma dragged her bike out of the shed and set off to the nearest chemist, half a mile through Medwell on the outskirts of the town.

'Serve him right,' she said to herself, grimly pedalling uphill with the sweat pouring into her eyes. But as soon as she had uttered this incantation the triumph left her soul as if the words had broken a spell.

Poor Howard. Poor, poor Howard. It wasn't his fault that everything happened to him. Nobody had ever looked after him properly. It wasn't his fault.

When she returned with her remedy in a bottle she led her husband, subdued and anxious in case he should be observed coming from the greenhouse clad only in a towel, to the bathroom where she tenderly deloused him.

By the time the children arrived home tea was ready and Howard was mending the refrigerator light which had refused to go on when the door was opened. He was wearing a clean pair of summer slacks and felt, as well as superficial tinglings, a deep sense of purification.

'Hello, Dad. We've been to Uncle Fred's. Flora's had six kittens, Mum. One of them's a ginger tom. Uncle Fred says we can have it, if you say yes. Say yes, Mum,' Andrew implored. 'Oh, you've had a bonfire,' he added looking out with disappointment at the last smoulderings of a conflagration in the garden.

'Just a few bits and pieces,' said Howard hastily.

'Mrs Tattersall was there with a Canadian lady who was drunk. Frances drew me a picture of Uncle Fred's calf. Look. Uncle Fred didn't seem very pleased to see us. I expect he was too hot. It's hot, isn't it? Are you hot, Dad?' Karen asked.

'Well, you'll be cooler when you've eaten this nice tea your mother's made. Wash your hands and sit down.' Howard was in charge again.

'What about the kitten, Mum?'

'Yes, you can have the kitten, when it's old enough to leave its mother,' said Thelma.

After all, it would be less trouble than a baby.

40

❦

'Well, just a little sniff,' said Freda. 'Just one more little sniff. It's not a long walk home.'

It was the evening before the departure of the two elderly ladies to visit Freda's relatives in Exeter. They were going for a week. Hermione had booked a double room with two single beds for them in a four-star hotel, having ensured, by her imperious manner over the telephone, that the beds would be dry, the food good and the service excellent.

They were having a farewell meal with William and Frances as Freda would be going straight from Exeter back to London to catch her plane home at the end of the week.

They started the meal with sherry. Hermione had been prevailed upon to drink one glass of this. Then they proceeded to wine. Hermione had drunk one glass of this. William and Freda had drunk another one and a half bottles between them. Frances, as usual, was drinking tea. She had made an extra effort to cook something nice and the chicken, if not cordon bleu, was edible.

'Do your relatives know that you and Hermione are coming to visit them?' William asked. Hermione had been trying without success to persuade Freda to telephone them for a fortnight.

'No, I guess not,' replied Freda with a little giggle.

There was a pause.

'Perhaps it would be a good idea to let them know. Then they would be expecting you,' William suggested.

'Well, no. I don't really like them,' Freda explained. 'They're just waiting for me to die.'

This seemed to be a good time for some more wine. Freda and William finished the second bottle.

One glass of sherry and one glass of wine had given a touch of luminosity to Hermione's nose and she and Freda sang a couple of verses of 'O, Canada'.

When the meal was over they had a small drop of liqueur. Because William couldn't find the liqueur glasses they had to use the sherry glasses. This made it difficult for him to judge how much liqueur he was pouring and his generosity contributed to the events that followed.

By half-past ten it had become a very jolly party.

'Now, Freda, dear,' said Hermione, 'you and I have a long coach journey ahead of us tomorrow. I think we had better go next door and retire to our beds.'

'Yes,' replied Freda, 'but I shall be retiring to your bed and you will be retiring to your pallet.' She gave a giggle which transformed itself into a hiccough.

Hermione had not slept properly for a fortnight. The Victorian chaise longue had given way to its baser instincts every time she turned over during the night, pinching whichever parts of her coincided with its arthritic joints. To make matters worse, Freda only slept for two hours at a time, and when she wasn't asleep she would get up and come downstairs to make a cup of coffee or look for some of the old newspapers to read, waking Hermione if she had happened to doze off for a moment or two.

It didn't really seem like a restful prospect, retiring to their beds. So they stayed for another half hour and had another drop of liqueur. Like many people who govern themselves according to strict rules, Hermione forgot the rules once they were broken. And she was very fond of liqueur. She had given William the Grand Marnier they were drinking for Christmas.

So when they were ready to set off for Hermione's cottage next door it was not surprising that the journey seemed perilous and that Freda's handbag couldn't be found.

'Are you sure you brought it with you?' Frances asked.

'Well, yes. I sure had it a little while or some time ago, back there.' Freda was becoming incoherent.

'Look under your chair.' Hermione was beginning to panic. There had been a lot of excitement. She needed some rest before the coach trip. The chaise longue suddenly seemed to invite her with the allure of a four-poster feather bed.

'No, it isn't there, that's for certain,' Freda announced, leaning forward to peer under her chair and coming to rest with her knees on the floor and her head on the sofa.

William righted Freda and they searched all around the kitchen table where they had eaten. It offered no clue as to the whereabouts of Freda's handbag. Of course, losing something in that house always presented a problem as one had to sort through so many things which were lost already.

Hermione made a sort of 'humphing' noise that an elephant makes when it is homesick.

'Freda, are you sure you brought it with you?' Her bonhomie was evaporating like the alcohol blazing away on top of a plate of crêpes suzettes.

'Sure, sure, sure, sure, sure,' Freda assured her. 'Sure.'

Taking another look under the armchair in which Freda had been enveloped in the sitting room William discovered an embroidered spectacle case containing Freda's spectacles.

'Were these in your handbag?' he asked her.

'Hooray. He's found my spectacles. Hermione, William has found my spectacles.'

'Were they in your handbag, Freda?' asked Frances.

'No. I just keep them for my nose.'

'Oh come on, Freda. We'll look at my house. You must have left it there.' Hermione stampeded through the front door as if she had caught a whiff of gunpowder. William and Frances and Freda followed her.

In Hermione's house everything was under control once more.

'Now William, you look in the kitchen. I'll look in here. Frances, go and look in the bathroom. Freda, see if you've left it in the bedroom.'

They all set off obediently.

After a few moments Freda's triumphant figure appeared, swaying, at the top of the stairs. She was brandishing the spectacle case over her head.

'I've found it. I've found it. All is not lost. I've found it,' she cried.

Hermione's hurricane broke.

'Freda,' she stormed. 'We're not looking for your spectacle case. We're looking for your handbag.'

By the time the vagrant handbag had been tracked down and William and Frances had gone home and Freda had settled drunkenly into Hermione's comfortable bed, the Victorian chaise longue seemed to welcome its occupant with uncharacteristic benevolence. She'd better make the best of it, anyway. It was going to be a long journey, and a long week, trying to keep track of Freda all by herself.

But, Hermione thought, as she adjusted delicate parts of herself to indelicate parts of the monstrosity she lay on, it had been a happy fortnight.

When she came home she would pay another visit to Yardale Farm, a place which reminded her of the truly gracious experiences of her youth and childhood with Clara and Elizabeth and poor dear Dad, when there had been no money so you didn't have to worry about whether you had it or not.

She must remember to ask that nice Mr Pickles to give her his sister's recipe for her date loaf. She would like to make one for him herself.

41

Joan possessed a very well-established defence mechanism. She was not lonely because she would not allow herself to admit that she was lonely. She had Martin. She had Alice and David. She had Thelma and she once had Howard. She had

Frances and she sometimes saw William, though he was a queer fish.

She knew most of the people in the village to nod to. She was not one for confiding in people, reciting her troubles. No. Joan was her own best friend. Since the early days of her marriage, in fact, by the time she was pregnant, she had known that she was going to end up alone, and she had.

Except for Martin. But you couldn't make too much of the bond between a mother and a child. It wasn't fair to the child. So she brought him up as well as she could without making too much fuss of him. He wasn't spoiled. He couldn't be spoiled in a material sense because Joan didn't have the money to indulge him. She didn't spoil him emotionally, either, though.

When she had first come to live in Medwell she had come because she could afford the very modest rent for her cottage, and because she wanted to get away from everything that reminded her of her marriage and that included her own family who had warned her that she was making a mistake.

She had always looked out for herself. When she began to work at the age of sixteen she had taken out an insurance policy which now that ten years had elapsed was due to mature. The premiums on this policy had been collected at the door of her cottage on the third day of each month for the past seven years by a shy, weary looking young man whom she knew only as Mr Worthington.

Mr Worthington was due to call this evening.

Joan had already cleaned the house from top to bottom, as she did every day. It was not that the house was dirty, or that she couldn't think of anything better to do. She enjoyed knitting and sewing. She had a few records and an old record player that she had bought at the flea market.

Because she had her three cleaning jobs which she went off to on alternate days she spent most of her time cleaning.

It was as if by washing and scrubbing and vacuuming and polishing she could take away from the fabric of herself the ugly stain of those two years of marriage, when she had been still a child, but a child subjected to the worst degradations that can be inflicted upon a woman. She would not allow herself to remember those years.

She put Martin's Lego away in a drawer at the bottom of the wooden cupboard built into the thick wall of the cottage by some humble weaver a hundred years ago. She straightened her pile of knitting patterns and made sure that the kettle was filled and the jam sponge ready on a plate.

Mr Worthington always had a mug of coffee and a piece of jam sponge. He called on her last thing before he went home, arranging his round thus to ensure that he would be able to enjoy his visit to Joan.

Tonight he was going to hand over the cheque.

Joan went into the garden. Her cottage was built into the hillside so that she had no back door. Above it, another neighbour's house sat against the back of her upstairs rooms and its door faced the road, while beside her David and Alice, who owned both the cottage at the back and the one on the roadside had two doors. Joan's large kitchen-living room downstairs and her two tiny rooms and little bathroom upstairs satisfied her well. It was a big enough house for the two of them.

She wandered past the heavy, drooping roses and chose four dark red ones which looked sleepy, drugged perhaps by their own strong perfume. She took them into her kitchen and arranged them in a bowl at the centre of the old, scrubbed table. Then she sat down to wait, as she had waited every month for the past seven years. She had waited for Mr Worthington because to her he represented security. She had little money and few possessions. But she had known that when her insurance policy matured she would have a little extra money and that she would be able to make her home more comfortable with some of it. She had waited for this day.

And this day had come.

Mr Worthington had not collected her widow's mite all these years without realising what it represented.

Martin was asleep in bed.

Joan had taken a bath and changed into her best cotton

dress. She was proud of this dress. She had bought the material, a fent, from one of the mill shops and it had cost her eighty pence. She had adapted an old pattern, giving the dress a deep neckline instead of its original prim round one. This exposed the warm space between her motherly, sunburned breasts. The skirt fitted well over her wide hips and fell in a feminine line which concealed her rather large thighs. Her short straight hair shone. She looked wholesome and clean and fresh.

In her kitchen the smells of a variety of soaps and detergents mingled with the overpowering scent of the four dark roses in a curious olfactory sonata of hygiene and abandonment.

She picked up her knitting. Behind the rookery on the hill the sky was red. She would see him pass the window. She dropped a stitch, peering anxiously as she attempted to retrieve it in the failing light.

He was there. He tapped quietly on the half-open door and she met him in a warm sunset glow of achievement and mutual recognition.

'Ah, Mrs Shuttleworth,' the young man mumbled. He had the look of a traveller condemned to go on and on.

'Come in, Mr Worthington.' Joan was joyful.

'The great day, Mrs Shuttleworth,' said Mr Worthington in a tired voice.

'Oh, the excitement.'

They stared at each other.

'Well, come in, come in.' Joan recalled her duties as a hostess.

'I will. Thank you.' Mr Worthington stepped into the kitchen and breathed deeply. A feeling of calm drifted over him as if he had been standing on a small island and the sea and other shores had been hidden from him by some wonderful luminosity.

Mr Worthington was accustomed to collecting money from people who had very little. He saw a great many threadbare establishments. He also visited better-off homes. But nowhere on his whole route did he find the utter peace of this household.

He sat down at the table and opened his tattered briefcase.

'I'll switch the light on. It's going to be dark soon.' Joan fussed about. She took two of the pretty flowered mugs out of the cupboard and put the kettle on the gas stove. She put a spoonful of instant coffee into each mug and took a small milk jug out of the refrigerator.

Mr Worthington tried to pull himself together.

'Now, there are one or two things for you to sign,' he said.

If only he could forget about all this: documents, premiums, money. If only he could just sit here. If only he could just sit here for ever, embraced by this place which he only allowed himself to think about for two days before and two days after the third day of each month.

Joan had been looking forward to this moment for so long. Now that it was here she realised that the money did not matter. She did not feel pleased that at last she would have a little nest egg. She did not feel triumphant that as well as managing she had saved something for a rainy day.

She felt pleased because she had saved something for a rainy day with Mr Worthington.

Mr Worthington consulted a pile of papers. He added up a few figures and wrote a number on a piece of paper. He looked at it for a few moments.

'Five hundred and sixty-five pounds and forty-three pence,' he said quietly.

Joan made the coffee. She cut two slices of the jam sponge.

'Well.' She put Mr Worthington's coffee in front of him and gave him a plate for his cake. 'Well, it's only money.' She sat down at the other side of the table. 'I mean, it's only money, isn't it?'

Mr Worthington looked at her in the lamplight. He knew that she had made the lampshade herself, as she had made the cushions for the two armchairs, the tea-cosy embroidered with a bright red and yellow bird on the shelf below the cupboard, the calendar with pressed flowers, the raffia baskets in which the plant pots with geraniums stood on the windowsill, the plaited rugs on the composition floor.

He felt a sudden need to cry.

He had needed to cry when they had told him that his

mother had been killed by a car on her way home from work. He had needed to cry then. But he had been fourteen years old. And he knew that he must not allow himself to cry. His mother had brought him up alone and they had never needed to cry. Somehow he would manage without her. And he still would not cry.

Now, as he ate Joan's sponge cake and drank Joan's coffee out of the mugs on which she had painted flowers to hide the stark white crockery, he knew that it was over.

'Mrs Shuttleworth,' he said. 'Mrs Shuttleworth, I'm so sorry.'

Joan walked towards him out of the light into the shadows behind his chair.

'That's all right, lad,' she said. 'You cry.' She put her arms around him and held his head against her best dress. 'It's all right. Don't you worry. We'll be all right. We'll manage, between us. We'll manage all right. The three of us. The likes of us always do.'

42

Albert hadn't seen Frances for several days. She had told him that William was away again. But every time he telephoned her she was out. He knew that Hermione, too, was away. It seemed a crying shame to be missing time that they could have spent doing things without the fear of the military tattoo of Hermione's knock on the door or one eye on the clock to be home in time to make William's tea. Exasperated, he dialled her number.

'This is Frances,' Frances said.

'I know it's bloody Frances,' Albert replied. 'Where have you been? I've been trying to reach you for three days.'

Frances sat in her kitchen with the telephone receiver pressed against her ear. A puzzled expression took over her countenance as an olive green sky before rain takes over the colour of the landscape.

'I don't know,' she said at last. 'I don't know where I've been. What day is it?'

'It's Thursday, all day.' Albert was trying to keep his patience. She was absolutely hopeless. What day is it? How could anyone not know what day it was. 'Look,' he said, allowing his pleasure at the sound of her voice to overcome his incredulity about her vagueness, 'look, it's another beautiful day. Let's go to Hardcastle Crags and paint the stream.'

'That would be lovely. I'll get my things together.'

Albert was himself again.

'O.K., Gorgeous. I'll be there in twenty minutes. Put your cami-knickers on,' he advised.

He didn't know why he did it. He couldn't understand why he found it so necessary to see Frances. It was ridiculous. Quite ridiculous. Not seeing her for a few days made him ache like a young bullock. A man of his age. He didn't know what his ham friends would say about it if they knew. In his long discussions over the radio he never mentioned that he had a woman friend, or that the painting expeditions which he described to them included somebody else. In fact, as he had only taken up amateur radio operating since his wife died and he had never spoken about his wife he supposed that many of his radio friends would assume that he was a bachelor who had no interest in women. Nor had he, at least not in women in general. He had been very close to his wife and had nursed her devotedly for many years. Frances had not taken her place. She simply, well, he didn't really know what she did. Frances was Frances, that was all.

He filled the big thermos flask with coffee, pushed a packet of biscuits into the side pocket of his painting bag and set off in his car for Medwell.

Frances couldn't understand why she felt like this. She changed into a sundress which had no straps but clung to her body supported by a broad piece of elastic around her chest under her arms.

She put a record on the record player and sat swaying to its basic rhythm with a look of transcendental happiness. It was ludicrous. It was all ludicrous.

Why was it that in middle age she had discovered in Albert the emotional adventure which most humans experienced before they reached the age of twenty?

Of course, at the normal age of discovery she had been wedging the beginnings of her femininity into a yard and a half of shapeless navy-blue gabardine and insinuating not dreaming melodies but long columns of grammatical and ungrammatical Latin constructions into her squashed psyche.

When the forces at work in Albert and the forces at work in Frances met at the door of William's cottage, Hermione away in Exeter chasing Freda in and out of second-hand bookshops and around the Cathedral precincts and William visiting a steam-engine exhibition taking place in Leeds conveniently close to the venue of his conference, it seemed necessary to express at once some of the power that had built up.

They hastened to the small room which belonged to Frances alone. Frances stretched out like a fern opening in the sunlight. Albert hurled himself at the bed.

Afterwards, the earth staggered to its feet drunk with the astonishment of unlikely passion. It had been swept momentarily off course. Its fields, hills, trees, birds and flowers had assumed an extra, awry brilliance.

Frances looked at her lover lying beside her wearing the face of an amused angel. But there was something else. There was something unusual about today. She couldn't think what it was.

Then she realised.

'Albert,' she said wisely, 'we are never too old for new experiences. This is the first time you have ever made love to me with your hat on.'

43

Alice knew that it was all true. What Hermann Hesse had suggested about our fragmentary age was right. Of course, he wasn't referring to romance, but romance was part of the universality of experience. We were on the wrong course, making as we did like distressed mariners for the shores of material achievement, oblivious of the rocks in the sea which lay between us and that other, greater reality.

What more conclusive proof could she have than the emotional miracle contained in the precision of Joan's meta-morphosis.

It was as if a thousand apparently insignificant circum-stances had come about which found their way together in a convoluted union of strands like the separate wires along which the current of an electrical impulse flows. It was as inexplicable as the great Creation, as wonderful, as profound.

That Joan, sturdy, steady Joan, should suddenly take in the man from the Prudential would have seemed impossible if one had thought of it. Yet it had happened.

Of course, Alice had seen him passing occasionally on the third day of the month to collect Joan's premiums. On his way to Joan's door he had to take the right of way which meant crossing their common patio outside her window. But who would have thought the time would come when he would be setting off across the patio each day to work and crossing it again each evening to rejoin his beloved?

It was all too romantic and beautiful to assimilate. One did not believe that such things really happened.

'Alice,' said Marcus, glancing up from his book, 'do you think it was wrong of me to look for the source?'

Alice concentrated the engines of her brain on the small mind.

'Why are you wondering, petal?' she asked.

'Well, I just thought it might not have been such a good idea.'

'It made us worry, wondering where you were, that's true,' said Alice.

'No, not that.'

'What then?'

Marcus spread his hands out, one across each of the open pages of his book and peered at them through his spectacles.

'More because I thought it would be special. And it wasn't. If I hadn't been and found it, I could have gone on thinking it was special for ever.'

Alice understood. Once you had found out about something you had to turn to something else. Finding out was like closing the door as you left a room in which you had been happy. Marcus had been less enthusiastic about the stream recently.

'Perhaps you didn't notice the special things because you didn't realise they were connected with the stream,' she suggested.

'Like what?' asked Marcus.

'Well.' Alice thought hard. 'It was really a very special thing that Albert happened to be there when you needed him. He wasn't out looking for you but he found you.'

'But he's not a hobbit.'

'No. He's not a hobbit. He paints good pictures, though, don't you think? You like your picture of the rocks, don't you?'

'Oh yes. It's a very good picture. It's a special picture. It makes the source look special. Even though it wasn't.'

'Perhaps Albert could see what was special because he wasn't looking for it. I mean, perhaps if, instead of looking for what you couldn't see, you looked harder and more carefully at what you could see, you would have seen something special.'

Marcus closed his book. He put it on the table. He walked into the other room and lay down on the sofa, covering the yellow angel.

Hadrian came through from the garden.

'What's up with Marcus the Maggot?' he asked his mother.

'Shh, don't disturb him, lovely. He's thinking.'

Endymion came through from the garden.

'Maggot is lying on the sofa,' he announced. 'Is it supper time yet? Martin's new dad is making a run for the rabbits, so that they can play in the grass without going all over the gardens. Martin's new dad has to sleep in Joan's room. They've only got two bedrooms. He could have come to live with us. We've got hundreds. Martin's new dad is called James.'

'I like James,' said Hadrian. 'Dymmie was chasing me with a dead rook we found under the trees. James stopped him. He put it in the dustbin.'

'But I took it out again,' Endymion added.

'So James said that if it wasn't staying in the dustbin it must be buried. So we buried it. Joan gave us a cardboard box and James said that as Endymion was the one who didn't think it should stay in the dustbin, Endymion should dig the hole,' said Hadrian.

'So I dug a hole and James came out and said that a hole in the soil was a better idea than a hole in the lawn and made me fill it in again.' Endymion liked a bit of opposition.

'We gave it a nice funeral, under the rose bushes. We sang "Holy Night". Joan said it was a Christmas song, not a funeral song. But we chose it because we like Christmas.' Hadrian wore the look he wore when he had gone up a ladder and not down a snake.

Marcus returned to the kitchen.

'Alice,' he said, looking at his mother seriously. 'I've decided that a source is not necessarily at the beginning of something. You can find the source right where you are.'

Hadrian and Endymion looked at their brother.

Endymion tapped the side of his forehead with his fore-finger and screwed up his right eye.

Hadrian sighed.

'We had a good funeral, Marcus,' he said casually.

'That's it, Marcus, my love, you've got it.' Alice had the feeling that there was something else on her mind. 'Oh yes,' she said, 'shall we have toasted cheese? Daddy will be back from his meeting soon. We could surprise him. He likes toasted cheese.'

'He likes football, too,' said Endymion, taking the cheese out of the refrigerator before his mother had time to forget about it again.

44

When William was away Frances was not prepared for being awake by being awakened before she woke up. Therefore she had an extended length of time in which to become involved in dreams.

It was during one of these dreams that she accidentally came across the answer to the apparently unanswerable question of how she was going to spend the rest of her life or the rest of Hermione's life, whichever proved to be the shorter, in the house next door to that cantankerous gentlewoman.

Frances was walking across the moor. It was one of those days when the light seems to make physical objects uncertain. The turf seemed not warm and solid but a mist of gold rising from nowhere and merging with the trees, rocks, hills and finally being drawn, attenuated and mystical, into the deep consciousness of the distant sky.

So she was not sure, when she noticed a small figure plodding ahead of her, whether this figure was a human form or an animated trick of the light. She hurried and came closer to it.

As she approached she could see that it was carrying a large grey polythene dustbin bag into which it was pushing paper wrappers, empty tins and coke bottles as it went along.

'Just look at all this rubbish,' puffed Hermione. 'How does it get here?'

'The wind blows it,' said Frances, feeling the sense of depressed frustration which always descended upon her when Hermione was looking at the muck she was standing in instead of at the stars overhead. Though of course, it was only a few Mars Bar wrappers and there weren't any stars, just white clouds glowing like shampooed sheep crossing the firmament in a multitude of disguises.

'No discipline. Nobody has any discipline these days.' Hermione ignored her daughter's reply to a query which was in any case only an expression of her innate fury.

They traversed the moor together as they traversed the years, aware that they were annoying each other intensely but even here, where they were apparently alone for ever, unable to rid themselves of either the annoyance or the unrecognised satisfaction it gave to them.

'There's the Mayor,' cried Frances. 'Let's go and talk to him.'

Hermione tucked her dustbin bag tidily behind a rock and straightened her skirt. She smoothed down the crest of her white hair which had been blown into a halo by the breeze and fluttered towards the stone wall which the elderly farmer was absorbed in mending.

'That nice Mr Pickles,' she said to nobody in particular.

Frances began to laugh. She didn't know why she was laughing. It simply seemed such a lovely state of affairs, the sunshine, the mysterious illumination, the Mayor working with age-old skills at the age-old task of rebuilding an age-old wall that stretched over the landscape like a piece of ex-hausted elastic, drawing the three of them into eternal vistas of heaven and hell.

'Aha, the ladies,' said the Mayor, courteously removing the navy-blue bobble hat he was wearing in spite of the heat.

'Good morning, my Lord,' said Hermione, crossing herself.

Frances was getting confused. She had supposed that the greeting was made in deference to the Mayor's imaginary status. But his imaginary status had evidently been elevated considerably in Hermione's mind.

'I've lived a good life and done everything that the nuns told me to,' said Hermione unctuously, giving a little curtsey.

'Well done, thou good and faithful servant,' said the Mayor. 'Now come along and I'll show you the ropes.'

With the air of an ancient don clad in cap and gown in an arched lecture hall the Mayor began to expound the mysteries of dry-stone walling. His lecture lasted for several seconds, or had it been hours, weeks, months, years, or had they ever done anything else, ever in the whole of eternity, but listen respectfully as Fred Pickles told them about headstones, copings, face stones, top stones, heartings and the intricacies of balter.

'Now, you'll need these.' The Mayor handed Hermione and Frances each a walling hammer and a pair of goggles. 'Go slow and steady like. There's no need to rush at it arse over tit. These hills were here before us all and they'll be here after us and when you reach yon top it'll all clear up.'

Hermione assumed the expression of total capitulation which she kept only for occasions on which she was doing the Lord's work specifically. Frances, vaguely aware that she was dreaming, realised that a lifetime's dedication to the moment when she would meet her Maker had paid off for Hermione. Here she was with Him now, not realising that it was only the Mayor, taking instructions for the rest of forever as if she had been picking up a new crochet pattern.

She looked towards the skyline. She knew that when they reached it the view from what now seemed the end would be the same as it was from here. The top to which Fred alluded was like the oasis the lost traveller in the desert sees tragically clearly in an illusion which is always just beyond his reach.

This was what it had all been leading up to. This was what the conflict had been about. It had all been in preparation for rebuilding a wall which had no beginning and no end. Rebuilding a wall with Hermione, from now until . . .

Frances realised with a shock that the terrible life she had led had brought her to this. For her this was the nature of hell. For Hermione, however, having a constructive task to perform and an excuse to bully, criticise and instruct her daughter while they performed it, presented quite a different prospect.

She looked glumly at the Mayor.

The Mayor, stroking his beard with an appreciative glance at Hermione's matronly bosom, gave Frances a wink.

Happily for Frances, her subconscious, having ceded this awful prospect, did not pursue it.

They were in the Mayor's kitchen – Frances, Hermione, Fred, the cat Flora, which for some reason now only had one eye, and a large, untidy, unidentified nun.

Aunt Clara was there too.

With a cry of joy Frances flung herself upon Aunt Clara, who was making currant bread.

Aunt Clara wiped her expansive nose with her floury arm, leaving a stray particle of dough on its tip.

'Wal, honey. Wal, whaddaya know. And my little Minny, too.' Aunt Clara rubbed the dough off her nose and Frances, deeply asleep in the morning sunlight of the bedroom with her face in her pillow, feeling the comfort and assurance of Aunt Clara's abundant embrace, remembered in some twilit recess those glowing Canadian years of childhood when the bombing of England and the threat of a Nazi-dominated world had been kept at bay by the unassailable ferocity of this woman's love. Aunt Clara included Hermione in the womb of her arms and to the dismay of Frances, Hermione burst into tears.

'Momma,' she sobbed. 'Momma.'

Aunt Clara's bread was being inspected by Flora. Frances, making a mental note that she must be careful when eating the currant bread in case there was any connection between the presence of currants and the fact that Flora's left eye was now missing, realised, for the first time in her life, that her mother had been an orphan.

She woke up in the silent house, sweat pouring from her body, down her chest, down her shoulders.

Hermione had been an orphan. Hermione's father, good-natured and ineffectual, had not given her any sense of security. Her mother had died when she was five. Elizabeth had been of the same temperament that she herself had developed, critical, conscious of status and social importance, dedicated more to the arts of society than to the art of loving the human race.

And as if that had not been enough, Hermione had come to England at the age of twenty-one as the bride of the wealthy young George and been given the responsibility of that complex household.

No wonder Hermione had been hard to make friends with. Hermione was still looking for her mother.

Frances woke up properly and went downstairs in her dressing gown to make the morning's first pot of tea. She felt as if she had been partially run over by a steamroller.

But the parts which had escaped were fluttering about with joyous cries, flying here and there as if exploring an unknown world in which cages do not exist. The answers to questions so important that they made the difference between heaven and hell had dropped from the tree, ripe, glowing, ready to nourish.

Frances felt the hatred from the peach changing back into the taste of fruit.

Of course Hermione had not wanted her to touch the baby. If you touched the baby you became attached to it. If you touched the baby you loved it, as she had loved that lost, faded Momma. And what you loved was taken from you.

Hermione's strictures had been designed to keep her children away from the danger of separation and loss.

The part of Hermione which was Aunt Clara was constantly straining against this sense of loss. She had lost Aunt Clara who was the next best thing to that faded momma, she had lost the magical land of her birth and her childhood, she had lost her young womanhood almost as soon as it had begun, she had lost her father who, unlike her husband George, had not been the provider of an establishment of everlasting felicity for his children.

Frances poured her fourth cup of tea, crying tears of

understanding and sympathy into it. She felt an overwhelming sense of loss herself.

She wished that Hermione had been next door instead of in Exeter with Freda. She longed to hear her mother's angry knock at the door, her customary complaints about the drains, the litter, the shortcomings of her neighbours. She wanted above all to provide Hermione with the mother that she had been looking for all her life, to give back to the Aunt Clara in Hermione what the real Aunt Clara had given to Frances herself when she had been a temporary orphan. Surely the Aunt Clara in Hermione must recognise and respond to this shoreless continent of love.

A tide of panic rushed over the pebbled beach of her new consciousness. Supposing Hermione dashed into Exeter High Street in pursuit of Freda and was killed by a car? She would never know that Frances understood. She would never know that her ban on touching the baby didn't matter.

She would never know that Frances had always touched the baby and that the baby had never been taken away from her.

Frances, who was never sure how to relate what was happening in her imaginary landscape to what was happening to everyone else, consulted the morning paper and compared its date with the notes in William's handwriting on the calendar. She discovered that William would be home tonight and that Hermione was due home in three days' time.

She would surprise them both. It was now late in the morning. But she would spend the rest of the day making her house beautiful and then she would prepare to tell Hermione, her mother, that she understood; that it didn't matter how she reacted to the village, to her daughter, that her daughter and the village would give her in return their warm affection and a more constructive attempt to see things from her point of view.

Anyway, perhaps it was time something was done to improve the drains.

45

❦

Frances had expected her mother to return from Exeter limp and exhausted. But she was wrong.

Having to keep an eye on Freda as though she had been a bright toddler, being thrown upon her own resources in the way of discovering entertainments for her, and not losing her friend, had recharged Hermione's batteries wondrously. It was a new experience for her. When she had been responsible for real toddlers there had always been Nanny to do the donkey-work.

She had not been humbled by her new experience. On the contrary. If she could manage alone in a strange city at her age with a wayward seventy-year-old there was no reason why young mothers should find it hard work coping with their offspring.

However, if she were to be honest about it, living in a four-star hotel during her first run in the role of nanny had made the job easier. Also, the rejuvenated feeling she had upon her return to the North was partly brought about by the knowledge that she would be able to sleep in her own comfortable bed again. Even a dry bed in a good hostelry didn't provide the comforts of home when it was situated three feet away from another one containing Freda whose two-hourly periods of sleep never coincided with the moments when Hermione managed to doze off. These always happened just before it was time for Freda to switch on the light and go walkabout. As well as her own bed there was another visit to Yardale Farm to look forward to. That nice Mr Pickles had been most pressing in his invitation, whispered urgently into her ear as she had prepared to steer Freda back down the lane with that impossible Alice and Frances and all those dreadful children at the end of the last visit.

So Hermione returned home in a good mood and was surprised to find a change in Frances. Not only had Hermione's own cottage been dusted and filled with flowers, and Freda's bed linen changed, but her daughter's house too had been transformed.

Hermione did wish, though, that Frances wouldn't keep looking at her in that strange way. It gave her a very uncomfortable feeling. Also, she had noticed, Frances was trying to get something out of her. Talking about her childhood to the Mayor was one thing. To the Mayor she felt she could confide her past, knowing that he would understand, and certain that he would never disclose what she divulged to another soul. Whereas Frances, who talked all day long to everyone she met about everything that crossed her mind, might pass on any information she accidentally imparted to – well, to almost anyone, even perhaps to that Mr . . . er . . . to that man who was always sitting in her kitchen drinking tea. She was perplexed, too, about her daughter's motive. Frances had never shown any interest in her mother's childhood before. Now, all at once, she was plying her with questions. How old had Aunt Clara been when their mother died? How had they been provided for if their father didn't have a job? What could she remember about it? It was quite upsetting.

The fish man hadn't called. It was tiresome to say the least. She had nothing for tomorrow's lunch. That meant she would have to telephone Nigel and ask him to bring her something from town, or walk over the hill to the shops. It was such a pull back up again. She was too old to have to walk all that way. Up the lane in the other direction was a different matter, especially now that she knew she could head for the Mayor's farm. She supposed that Frances had forgotten to ask him to call. Frances had a memory that was about as reliable as the weather. You couldn't even rely on the weather to be terrible. Look at this glorious summer.

Hermione went to her daughter's house to ask whether she was sure that she had asked the fish man to call. She knocked on the door as if she expected it to be opened by the Speaker of the House of Commons.

Frances peered intently at her mother.

'If Aunt Elizabeth was going to get married, what did they do about you?' she enquired, resuming the conversation where they had left it last time they met.

'Clara looked after me, of course,' snapped Hermione. 'You don't think I could have been taken off to live with a couple of newlyweds, do you?'

'You must have felt a nuisance. In the way, I mean,' said Frances.

'Of course I felt a nuisance. I was in the way. Clara was only sixteen. She was being courted by Uncle Sam. Father had his own fish to fry. Of course I felt a nuisance. I was a nuisance.' Hermione was getting angry.

They were now sitting at the kitchen table. Hermione tapped rhythmically on its surface with her fingers.

Something at the back of her mind told Frances that now was the time to stop. Hermione did not want to remember. But something nearer to the front of it told her to go on.

'Can you remember your mother?' she asked.

It was the nearest thing to cruelty that she was capable of. Marcus would have said that sometimes you have to be cruel to be kind. This was what she intended. Hermione's psychological boil needed to be lanced.

'Yes,' Hermione replied simply, 'yes, I can.'

There was a long pause. Hermione had stopped tapping the table.

Frances could hear the clock ticking. She had bought it in a junk shop. It possessed a commanding and melodious chime which it indulged every quarter of an hour. Unfortunately it didn't keep good time and to compensate for this failing it sometimes chimed a double-chime between the quarters which could be startling. Frances sat on the edge of her chair, wondering which would come next, an explosion from her mother or a campanological offering from the clock.

'Clara once told me, when I was grown up, of course,' said Hermione quietly, realising as she said it that she had gone too far but that she couldn't stop now, 'Clara once told me that she held me in her arms downstairs while Momma was dying upstairs.'

They sat in silence, the mother and the daughter.

The clock, realising that this was an historic moment, ploughed on towards the next quarter without testing its bells.

'Think of it. Two young girls stuck at sixteen and eighteen with a five-year-old sister and no mother. However could they manage?'

Hermione put her head in her hands and wept.

'Momma. Poor Momma.'

Frances thought she was having déjà vu. She felt the same dismay that she had felt in her dream.

But this time instead of waking she stood up and put her arms around her mother.

'Well, Mum,' she said sensibly, 'they did manage, didn't they, and a very good job they made of you, I'd say.'

As she held the sturdy, compact shape of Hermione she realised that she had never before in her whole life addressed her mother as 'Mum'. She also realised that nothing could ever be as bad between them again.

'Yes,' said Hermione wiping her eyes, 'I'd say so too. They made a good job of me.' She bent down and picked up a stray newspaper off the kitchen floor and put it tidily into the waste bin. 'Now. About this fish man. Are you sure you asked him to call? I've waited in for him all day. It's very inconsiderate. Tradespeople don't even try to be obliging any more. In the old days you knew that if they said they would call, they would call. I don't know what the world's coming to. It's every man for himself. And don't spare the horses.'

Frances looked at Hermione and Hermione looked at Frances.

They knew that there had been something wrong with this last pronouncement, but neither of them could have said what it was.

They both laughed.

It was a joke, not an English joke which Hermione could not understand, but a joke of the kind that Aunt Clara might have made, though she would have made it inadvertently too.

It was within the sphere of Aunt Clara's influence, accessible to them both.

It didn't need to be explained.

46

❧

'I've been telling them for months. I've been telling everybody. I've told Frances. It's rice and tea leaves. Now look what's happened.' Hermione stood with the rest of the village looking down into the hole in the road.

'Still, better than the shite-cart,' Aunt Ella mused, standing beside Hermione, not having heard what she said but having correctly surmised that she had been complaining about the drains.

'This has nothing to do with tea leaves and rice,' Frances protested reasonably. 'This is the sewer.'

'A blockage is a blockage. Pipes can only take so much,' said Hermione piously.

At the foot of the metal ladder at the bottom of the hole Howard pushed the last of a third set of drain rods into the constipated drain. Then he scrambled up the ladder towards the posy of faces nodding down at him from the road.

'More rods,' he gasped as he reached the surface. He took a deep gulp of air and disappeared back into the depths.

'More rods. He wants more rods,' the word passed among the crowd.

David handed on another bundle of rods which Aunt Ella's Tom had fetched from his farm as news that the main sewer was out of action had reached the outskirts of the village.

'Used to come once a month, the shite-cart,' Aunt Ella explained to Hermione. 'Sucked it all out of the privvies. Sloshed through the back field. Even the cows couldn't stand it. Trudged right over to the other side of the hill when it appeared. Especially in hot weather.' Aunt Ella raised her voice to ensure that Hermione would hear her.

Howard was wearing a navy-blue beret with a leather band around its rim to protect him from the obvious hazards of being in amongst the sewage. The navy-blue beret popped out of the hole above Howard's strangely-hued countenance as he exhaled like a whale and took another deep breath before descending once more. The smell from the hole was becoming overpowering even in the street.

Taking up an authoritative position between Hermione and the hole and with an arm outstretched protectively to prevent anyone from falling in on top of Howard, the Mayor addressed his brother-in-law.

'Now then,' he shouted down the hole, his voice rebounding against the slimy brick sides of the pit, 'now then, our Howard, don't get carried away. All them rods has to come back out again, you know. We don't want you drowned in a log jam when she frees.'

He smiled comfortably, aware of Hermione's eyes upon the back of his head.

As his words reached the bottom they were submerged in a roaring tide which began far below their feet and rose to a glutinous crescendo, shattering the attentive silence as the watchers took a sharp breath in unison.

'Stand back. There she goes,' commanded the Mayor.

James moved Joan gently away from the hole to a position of safety as the crowd tottered backwards, making way for Howard who was throwing out drain rods like a demented arsonist rejecting spent matches and clambering hurriedly up the metal ladder in their wake.

As he reached the surface the underground torrent, growling and slobbering, partially filled the hole behind him, then began to subside, making its way demurely into its appointed channels as if to indicate that it had not really meant to get him but had just been teasing.

Marcus, peering into the turgid gloom, commented with interest,

'It's full of balloons.'

The rest of the children joined him.

'Who's filled it with balloons?' they demanded in a chorus of indignation at this waste of a precious commodity.

The crowd trickled back to the edge of the hole. A little wave of admiring merriment started at the front and gathered strength as it lapped its way through the beholders.

'Ah, now then . . .' The Mayor, having inspected the balloons, cleared his throat and began to make shrewd calculations.

Number three was Joan and James. Judging by Joan's condition, they hadn't been using balloons. She'd make a good feeder, too, would Joan. Most certainly it would be on the breast, that one. And her James, a quiet lad but grand with the kiddies. He'd make a good dad. No, it wouldn't be number three.

Number five. Number five was Aunt Ella's. Out of the question. He looked slyly at Aunt Ella.

'I don't know what they're on about,' Aunt Ella shouted at Hermione. 'Did he find a body?'

'It's disgusting,' Hermione replied, averting her eyes from the hole and choosing to remain in ignorance.

But number seven.

The Mayor glanced across the open manhole at Alice whose Renaissance face was gleaming like the bottom of a copper pan caught by the evening sunlight, rosy as the trees on the hill behind them all whose leaves stirred languidly, crimson and ready to scatter on the autumn air.

Alice, rising above her embarrassment, thought how strange it was to see what had been consigned discreetly to the oblivious disposals of science and hygiene thus exposed in its glory.

So, no doubt, all secrets would one day be revealed in a blinding flash.

✿

47

It was three days before Christmas. The community had gathered for its annual singing of carols in the old school-room.

This year they had engaged the services of the Youth Band from the town. The young people were arranging themselves on the stage, assembling their instruments, while their young conductor, standing neat and self-possessed, dominated the whole of the crowded hall: slim and pretty, she seemed to be the only adult in command of herself and the occasion as she raised her music-stand and gave last-minute instructions in a quiet voice.

The old schoolroom was slightly damp and steamy. It had been snowing heavily and the village had turned up with snow on its boots which melted in pools and condensed into a cheerful consommé of droplets and germs. The ancient floorboards creaked with the weight of the villagers and the uncomfortable wooden benches, polished almost black by the backsides of generations of children, sagged under their festive occupants.

Fred Pickles looked appreciatively at the large flakes falling across the windows against the darkness outside, like a host of moths which had been supping-up and didn't rightly know where they were going.

Some months ago, at the end of the summer, he had bought himself an ancient Land Rover. This vehicle, though not as romantic as a tram, had proved useful, as he had hoped it would, in transporting Mrs Tattersall to Yardale Farm on her now frequent visits. She came of an evening and they sat, one on either side of the fire in the squashed armchairs. Among the treasures on Jeremiah's bookshelves Hermione had discovered a complete set of the works of Dickens. She had decided that it would be doing the Mayor a great service to read these to him and the project suited him down to the ground. They were in the middle of 'A Christmas Carol' at present.

After the concert he would take her back to the farm and she would continue with the story. Because of this assignation the Mayor was cherishing hopes of a really heavy snowstorm. For the past few weeks he had been keeping his mother's feather bed aired and warm in case of such an emergency and much of the time while Hermione was reading he spent in trying to think of ways in which he might manage to observe that magnificent bosom unclad as she prepared to accept refuge in the farm and climb into the cosy bed in which Agnes had died, after he had courteously bade her good-night and pretended to retire to his own.

He glanced sideways at her where she sat, pleasant as a robin, between him and William. As usual there were not enough copies of the carols to go around and he had gallantly given her his in the certainty that she would offer to share it with him when the time came to sing and he would have to move as close to her as he could get and bend over her well in order to read the words, as he had forgotten to bring his reading spectacles with him.

On the stage there was a sudden flurry of activity. The rest of the schoolroom was lit by four bulbs hanging from the ceiling by frayed wires. But the stage remained in semi-darkness. It had not occurred to anyone that the musicians, too, would require illumination. All the handymen of the village, David, Howard and James among them, were engaged in arguing about the best method of providing this amenity. They could, David suggested, use an extension lead which they could attach to the bent metal rail which was designed to hold the curtain at the front of the stage on those occasions when the curtain could be found.

Howard agreed about the usefulness of an extension lead, and one of the young men ran home to fetch his, but he also pointed out in basic terms that it was no good attaching it to the curtain rail.

The Mayor smiled indulgently. Something always went wrong. Christmas carols wouldn't be Christmas carols if you could just walk in and start to sing.

He looked at the black windows with deep satisfaction. They were heavily encrusted with snow, like ponds with ice around the edges, and the snow was still falling.

It was a mistake to count your chickens before they were hatched. The snow could stop and the sky clear, brittle and starry as a dome of frost, before the evening was out.

But if it didn't, tonight could be the night.

Thelma sat with Karen and Andrew and watched Howard as he explained to the others that if they attached the extension lead to the curtain rail, the light would only reach the first row of the musicians. She saw him point to a hook in the high ceiling over the centre of the stage, left, no doubt, from some Thespian venture of bygone days. She saw the handymen scrambling in and out of the youngsters in search of a ladder.

The musicians, sitting in the gloom, were now peering self-consciously at their familiar scores as if they were full of complications. They wished they could see properly. They wished they could begin so that the audience wouldn't be looking at them any longer.

As she observed how deftly Howard instructed the other men, how he was the first to climb the ladder which they eventually unearthed from a corner of the little kitchen, how cleverly he lassooed the extension lead over the hook when it arrived in the hands of its panting deliverer, Thelma felt a surge of pride.

He was her Howard, her man. He had been different since he had come home, less restless, more relaxed, more talkative, nicer to the children. He had also been different towards her, gentler, more demonstrative. He now behaved with a greater air of trust, as if, having tried her to the limit, he knew that he would be acceptable to her without the need to demonstrate his masculinity like an over-anxious peacock.

And at the end of the summer he had built the sunhouse outside the back door.

Thelma felt in her pocket and clasped a small box in which there lay a silver brooch wrapped in yellow cotton wool. She had gone to the flea market one Saturday and asked the jewellery-man whether he could find her something old for a friend of hers, knowing that something old would please Frances more than the kind of thing she might choose for herself. But the jewellery which he showed her, assuring her that it was Victorian, was exactly like some which her brother Fred had tried to give to her after the death of their mother. Agnes had treasured these objects but Howard had told Thelma that they were too old-fashioned to wear so they had remained in a drawer at the farm, undisturbed. From amongst them, Thelma had now chosen a brooch for Frances and she had waited until Christmas to give it to her. She planned to catch her before she went home after the carol service.

It did not occur to Thelma that Frances, like Thelma herself, had felt completely rewarded by Howard's return.

Thelma, sighing contentedly, thought of the petrol-blue taffeta skirt and the high-necked blouse she had bought to wear for the Christmas dinner party with her friends from the egg factory. (Howard insisted that she spend the money she earned on herself, and was appreciative of the results.) It didn't matter that they would be going without their respective spouses to the smart hotel. They would be seen by them before they left and after they returned. The fact that the men were excluded merely made the event more mysterious and delightful.

Howard, aware that his wife was looking at him, chatted with the young conductor, knowing that Thelma would never have to worry again about his being carried away by another woman, twenty and blonde though she might be.

James, standing by the door of the old schoolroom, waited for a signal to try the light switch.

Beside Thelma, Andrew sat very straight, fiddling with a piece of plasticene he had found in his pocket. He squashed it until it became pliable, then rolled it between his flat palms, making a phallus. He was glad his dad had come home. This was not only because he wanted to know that there would be somebody to look for him should he ever become lost, but also because a new relationship had sprung up between them. Though three years older than Marcus, he too had been unclear in his mind about the details of mating. Howard had taken him aside and explained it all, man to man, in a remarkably casual and comforting way. He had passed on some of this information to Marcus, but Marcus, whose thoughts always went off at a tangent, didn't seem to have absorbed it as completely as he might.

Sitting on the other side of Thelma, Karen looked up at her mother. She knew Thelma was happy again and this made her happy. She put her hand through her mother's arm and squeezed. She hoped the carols would begin soon. These benches were hard.

Karen noticed that Aunt Ella was sitting just in front of them. She hoped that she would manage not to laugh. Aunt Ella was always three lines behind everyone else when she sang. And her voice was as loud as a foghorn. Dad said it was rude to laugh at people. But it was awfully difficult not to. It came over you, like sneezing.

Endymion, sitting between Alice and the space which was waiting for David, thought about the box of matches in his pocket. He had borrowed it from Mr Todd's shop when Mr Todd was serving Alice. It had not been stealing because he would put it back the next time he went. He needed the matches to light his banger. The banger was in his other pocket. It was a bit tattered. He had saved it from bonfire night. He felt it with his right hand in his right pocket. A thrill of evil-doing went through his wiry frame. Of course, he wouldn't let it off near to anybody. That would be dangerous. David had made sure that they all understood how bad it was to throw fireworks or let them off in crowds. In fact, he had never lit a firework by himself, or with a match. On bonfire night they each had a piece of smouldering string and took it in turns to light them, closely supervised by David.

No. He would wait until they were all outside again. He would creep through the snow to the top of the pile left by the plough at the side of the road where they couldn't see him. Excitement mounted in his breast. What a joke it was going to be. They would think an avalanche was coming.

Endymion laughed out loud.

Alice, hearing his laughter, looked down at Endymion.

It was wonderful that children enjoyed the mystery of Christmas so much. They became engrossed in its magic. Perhaps magic wasn't the right word. It was mythology, or was it Truth. Perhaps she shouldn't let such questions into the portals of her mind at this moment.

At any rate, they became engrossed in its message of love and peace.

James, standing by the light switch, waited for the signal. The musicians had fallen into a kind of trance, thinking it would be Easter before all these men had finished messing about. Now they had discovered that the extension lead which Howard had so adroitly attached to the hook was too high up for them to fit a bulb into its socket.

Hadrian, on the other side of his mother, felt anxious. He counted. There were fourteen young people on the platform, without the lady conductor and the light crew. He knew from experience, having crawled under it looking for props when they were doing plays, that the stage was not built to launch a battleship. If the stage collapsed all these people, including his dad, could be hurt. His mind raced to the possibility of broken legs and arms. He knew that Father Christmas was only David dressed up. He had never let his mother know that he knew, because he didn't want to disappoint her. Nor had he told his younger brothers. But if David had a broken leg he wouldn't be able to creep round on Christmas Eve wearing a false beard and Alice's red dressing gown and filling the stockings. That would mean no presents, or at best, if David wasn't hurt too badly, the other two, seeing him with his arm in a sling for instance, would put two and two together, knowing that it would be too much of a coincidence that both he and Father Christmas should have broken an arm at the same time.

Hadrian sat transfixed with anxiety. He willed the light to work. He willed the men to get off the stage. He willed the carol singing to begin.

Marcus, sitting next to Hadrian, was peering through his owl-eye glasses at the nativity mural which ran the whole length of the old schoolhouse. The schoolchildren had painted it with Frances and her friend Albert Hobbit. There was the advent panel with the three kings travelling towards the star, the shepherds' scene with some pretty unusual-looking sheep, and the stable with Mary and Joseph, and the baby lying in a manger.

Marcus didn't think much of Karen's camels. He had told her that camels have two humps, that it is dromedaries who only have one, but she wouldn't listen to him. And the humps were bigger than the rest of the camels. That was just silly. Everybody knew that you couldn't have humps that were bigger than their camels. One hump bigger than its camel was not only inaccurate, it was ridiculous.

He sniffed. Things that had been got wrong irritated him. Not that the humps weren't carefully drawn and painted. They were. Karen was very neat. She didn't go over the edges. It was just that they were much too big, and there were not enough of them. Half as many as there should have been.

Transferring his attention to the manger scene he allowed his thoughts to wander to a preoccupation of his own. His mind was much clearer about the source of himself now. Andrew had explained how the seed met the egg and he was satisfied with the explanation, as far as it went. If it became hard it would be easy to plant with it. But the Holy Ghost. He was not at all sure about that. Joseph would have been all right. Marcus knew, though, that a ghost can't go hard. So what was the source of the baby Jesus? Why hadn't he begun the way everyone else did? He made a mental note to ask Alice about this on the way home. It obviously needed a good deal of thought.

Hermione wondered when they were going to get that wretched light working but she kept an agreeable smile fixed on her face, conscious of the Mayor at her side. It was annoying though. Why couldn't somebody have thought about a light for the band? Surely they must have realised that a musician can't read his music in the dark. It was always the same. Whatever happened in this village it always went off at half cock. She struggled with a mixture of feelings, her frustration at the inadequacy of the organisation and her strange contentment in the Mayor's proximity.

He had washed his beard, she noticed. It gleamed silver and pale red-gold and she caught a faint smell of something that she did not recognise as a well-known brand of after-shave lotion as advertised on the television. The Mayor had smoothed his cheeks between the beginnings of his beard and his handsome features with Jeremiah's razor which he had found in the old tobacco cabinet in the bathroom. Then he had rubbed this toilet preparation generously into his skin. One had to take these extreme measures for the ladies, he knew, though he had never been in this situation before.

In spite of herself, Hermione discovered that the benevolent emotions were winning. She thought about her hours in front of the Mayor's fire reading to him. When they had finished with Dickens they would start on Jeremiah's volumes of the works of Hugh Walpole. It gave her such pleasure to be able to enlarge the Mayor's mental landscape, giving him wider horizons which would brighten his sleepless nights.

Hermione, of course, did not know that the Mayor fell asleep as soon as his shaggy head touched the pillow and that he slept soundly until his alarm clock roused him in the morning. Nor did she know that towards the end of their evenings together, when the pleasure of scrutinising her pink countenance and her breathtaking bosom had begun to pall, the big man, his arms folded across his chest and his eyes closed, was not in fact listening with deep concentration but drowsing comfortably.

Noticing with pleasure that the handymen were trying to attract the attention of James who had let his vigilance slip at the light switch, Hermione cleared her throat and looked forward to the Mayor's surprise when he heard the virginal tones of her clear soprano voice ringing out like a Christmas bell.

A few rows further back Joan smoothed her winter coat over the bulge and peered down towards the front of the school-room to see whether Martin was behaving himself. He had run off to see whether James wanted any help.

Pregnancy suited her. She was young. She was healthy. She had already produced one child without too much difficulty. And she was riding on the white horse of love.

She looked across at James, standing ready by the switch. He caught her eye and she blushed, deep and dark as the four roses that had witnessed her marriage. Not the actual mar-riage, of course. That was still to come. Sometime in the spring, they thought. There was plenty of time.

James smiled back at her, noting her blush, noting her beauty, noting everything that had changed his world from a bleak world of wreckage to a world of tranquil reparation.

He pointed to the other side of the stage where Martin was unwrapping the extension lead from the leg of a stool it had become ensnared with, under the guidance of Howard.

Joan gave him a little thumbs-up sign and they gazed at each other over the heads of the gathering.

'James,' shouted David from the stage, 'lights, James.'

Falling to earth like an apple James switched on the light and the musicians were bathed in glory. The difficult part of the evening was over.

The handymen were all reunited with their families.

'Above thy deep and dreamless sleep
The silent stars go by . . .'
sang the community.

It had stopped snowing. The Mayor sighed. Still, it would be a right nice moonlit scene, from the Land Rover.

'How still we see thee lie . . .'
sang Aunt Ella, her voice round and fecund like the bellow of a bull.

Karen's shoulders began to shake.

Endymion scraped his fingernail along the sandpaper-edge of the matchbox in his pocket. Not long now.

The musicians, their eyes fixed on their scores, their cheeks red and huge, blew with gusto and the energy of Christmas filled the old schoolroom as the snow outside had filled every hollow, covered every snag, assuaged the earth with its generosity.

Frances looked up at William, who, like many a good atheist before him, was enjoying his Christmas chaunt. She could tell by the rapt expression on his face that he was thinking about steam engines.

Dear William. Dear, dear William.

This was her place. These were her people.

Here was her baby.

She looked at Joan, standing close to James, and the joy of creation brought tears to her eyes.

It wasn't just the baby in the nativity scene which they had made, though He might well have begun it all. It was the baby in everything that brought comfort and hope.

Hermione, enjoying the Mayor's astonishment at the loveliness of her voice, took a moment off to poke Frances in the back, around behind William, with an imperious finger.

'Sit up, Frances,' she hissed, 'you're slouching.'

Frances smiled at her mother and sat up.

Later on, when they had walked home through the snow under the black, star-crowded sky, William would go to the Friends of the Railways Club for a Christmas drink. And she would telephone Albert. He would come in his car and take her for a Christmas celebration in front of his fire.

None of this would improve the lot of the tormented world.

But if happiness could be acceptable by way of prayer, she would offer hers.